2.50
40502

A LOST LADY

A LOST LADY

BY

WILLA CATHER

"................. Come, my coach!
Good night, ladies; good night, sweet ladies,
Good night, good night."

VINTAGE BOOKS
A Division of Random House • New York

PART ONE

I

THIRTY or forty years ago, in one of those grey towns along the Burlington railroad, which are so much greyer today than they were then, there was a house well known from Omaha to Denver for its hospitality and for a certain charm of atmosphere. Well known, that is to say, to the railroad aristocracy of that time; men who had to do with the railroad itself, or with one of the "land companies" which were its by-products. In those days it was enough to say of a man that he was "connected with the Burlington." There were the directors, the general managers, vice-presidents, superintendents, whose names we all knew; and their younger brothers or nephews were auditors, freight agents, departmental assistants. Everyone "connected" with the Road, even the large cattle- and grain-shippers, had annual passes; they and their families rode about over the line a great deal. There were then two distinct social strata in the prairie States; the homesteaders and hand-workers who were there to make a living, and the bankers and gentlemen ranchers who came from the Atlantic seaboard to invest money and to "develop our great West," as they used to tell us.

When the Burlington men were travelling back and forth on business not very urgent, they found it agreeable to drop off the express and spend a night in a pleasant house where their importance was delicately recognized; and no house was pleasanter than that of Captain Daniel Forrester, at Sweet Water. Captain Forrester was himself a railroad man, a contractor, who had built hundreds of miles of road for the Burlington,—over the sage brush and cattle country, and on up into the Black Hills.

The Forrester place, as every one called it, was not at all remarkable; the people who lived there made it seem much larger and finer than it was. The house stood on a low round hill, nearly a mile east of town; a white house with a wing, and sharp-sloping roofs to shed the snow. It was encircled by porches, too narrow for modern notions of comfort, supported by the fussy, fragile pillars of that time, when every honest stick of timber was tortured by the turning-lathe into something hideous. Stripped of its vines and de-

nuded of its shrubbery, the house would probably
have been ugly enough. It stood close into a fine
cottonwood grove that threw sheltering arms to
left and right and grew all down the hillside
behind it. Thus placed on the hill, against its
bristling grove, it was the first thing one saw on
coming into Sweet Water by rail, and the last
thing one saw on departing.

To approach Captain Forrester's property, you
had first to get over a wide, sandy creek which
flowed along the eastern edge of the town.
Crossing this by the foot-bridge or the ford, you
entered the Captain's private lane, bordered by
Lombardy poplars, with wide meadows lying on
either side. Just at the foot of the hill on which
the house sat, one crossed a second creek by the
stout wooden road-bridge. This stream traced
artless loops and curves through the broad
meadows that were half pasture land, half marsh.
Any one but Captain Forrester would have
drained the bottom land and made it into highly
productive fields. But he had selected this place
long ago because it looked beautiful to him, and
he happened to like the way the creek wound
through his pasture, with mint and joint-grass and
twinkling willows along its banks. He was well
off for those times, and he had no children. He
could afford to humour his fancies.

When the Captain drove friends from Omaha or Denver over from the station in his democrat wagon, it gratified him to hear these gentlemen admire his fine stock, grazing in the meadows on either side of his lane. And when they reached the top of the hill, it gratified him to see men who were older than himself leap nimbly to the ground and run up the front steps as Mrs. Forrester came out on the porch to greet them. Even the hardest and coldest of his friends, a certain narrow-faced Lincoln banker, became animated when he took her hand, tried to meet the gay challenge in her eyes and to reply cleverly to the droll word of greeting on her lips.

She was always there, just outside the front door, to welcome their visitors, having been warned of their approach by the sound of hoofs and the rumble of wheels on the wooden bridge. If she happened to be in the kitchen, helping her Bohemian cook, she came out in her apron, waving a buttery iron spoon, or shook cherry-stained fingers at the new arrival. She never stopped to pin up a lock; she was attractive in dishabille, and she knew it. She had been known to rush to the door in her dressing-gown, brush in hand and her long black hair rippling over her shoulders, to welcome Cyrus Dalzell, president of the Colorado & Utah; and that great man had never felt more flattered. In his eyes, and in the eyes of the admiring middle-aged men who visited there, whatever Mrs. Forrester chose to do was "lady-like" because she did it. They could not imagine her in any dress or situation in which she would not be charming. Captain Forrester himself, a man of few words, told Judge Pommeroy that he had never seen her look more captivating than on the day when she was chased by the new bull in the pasture. She had forgotten about the bull and gone into the meadow to gather wild flowers. He heard her scream, and as he ran puffing down the hill, she was scudding along the edge of the marshes like a hare, beside herself with laughter, and stubbornly clinging to the crimson parasol that had made all the trouble.

Mrs. Forrester was twenty-five years younger than her husband, and she was his second wife. He married her in California and brought her to Sweet Water a bride. They called the place home even then, when they lived there but a few months out of each year. But later, after the Captain's terrible fall with his horse in the mountains, which broke him so that he could no longer build railroads, he and his wife retired to the house on the hill. He grew old there,—and even she, alas! grew older.

II

BUT we will begin this story with a summer morning long ago, when Mrs. Forrester was still a young woman, and Sweet Water was a town of which great things were expected. That morning she was standing in the deep bay-window of her parlour, arranging old-fashioned blush roses in a glass bowl. Glancing up, she saw a group of little boys coming along the driveway, barefoot, with fishing-poles and lunch-baskets. She knew most of them; there was Niel Herbert, Judge Pommeroy's nephew, a handsome boy of twelve whom she liked; and polite George Adams, son of a gentleman rancher from Lowell, Massachusetts. The others were just little boys from the town; the butcher's red-headed son, the leading grocer's fat brown twins, Ed Elliott (whose flirtatious old father kept a shoe store and was the Don Juan of the lower world of Sweet Water), and the two sons of the German tailor,—pale, freckled lads with ragged clothes and ragged rust-coloured hair, from whom she sometimes bought game or catfish when they appeared silent and spook-like at her kitchen door and thinly asked if she would "care for any fish this morning."

As the boys came up the hill she saw them hesitate and consult together. "You ask her, Niel."

"You'd better, George. She goes to your house all the time, and she barely knows me to speak to."

As they paused before the three steps which led up to the front porch, Mrs. Forrester came to the door and nodded graciously, one of the pink roses in her hand.

"Good-morning, boys. Off for a picnic?"

George Adams stepped forward and solemnly took off his big straw hat. "Good-morning, Mrs. Forrester. Please may we fish and wade down in the marsh and have our lunch in the grove?"

"Certainly. You have a lovely day. How long has school been out? Don't you miss it? I'm sure Niel does. Judge Pommeroy tells me he's very studious."

The boys laughed, and Niel looked unhappy.

"Run along, and be sure you don't leave the gate into the pasture open. Mr. Forrester hates to have the cattle get in on his blue grass."

The boys went quietly round the house to the gate into the grove, then ran shouting down the grassy slopes under the tall trees. Mrs. Forrester watched them from the kitchen window until they disappeared behind the roll of the hill. She turned to her Bohemian cook.

"Mary, when you are baking this morning, put in a pan of cookies for those boys. I'll take them down when they are having their lunch."

The round hill on which the Forrester house stood sloped gently down to the bridge in front, and gently down through the grove behind. But east of the house, where the grove ended, it broke steeply from high grassy banks, like bluffs, to the marsh below. It was thither the boys were bound.

When lunch time came they had done none of the things they meant to do. They had behaved like wild creatures all morning; shouting from the breezy bluffs, dashing down into the silvery marsh through the dewy cobwebs that glistened on the tall weeds, swishing among the pale tan cattails, wading in the sandy creek bed, chasing a striped water snake from the old willow stump where he was sunning himself, cutting sling-shot crotches, throwing themselves on their stomachs to drink at the cool spring that flowed out from under a bank into a thatch of dark watercress. Only the two German boys, Rheinhold and Adolph Blum, withdrew to a still pool where the creek was dammed by a reclining tree trunk, and, in spite of all the noise and splashing about them, managed to catch a few suckers.

The wild roses were wide open and brilliant, the blue-eyed grass was in purple flower, and the silvery milkweed was just coming on. Birds and butterflies darted everywhere. All at once the breeze died, the air grew very hot, the marsh steamed, and the birds disappeared. The boys found they were tired; their shirts stuck to their bodies and their hair to their foreheads. They left the sweltering marsh-meadows for the grove, lay down on the clean grass under the grateful shade of the tall cottonwoods, and spread out their lunch. The Blum boys never brought anything but rye bread and hunks of dry cheese,— their companions wouldn't have touched it on any account. But Thaddeus Grimes, the butcher's red-headed son, was the only one impolite enough to show his scorn. "You live on wienies to home, why don't you never bring none?" he bawled.

"Hush," said Niel Herbert. He pointed to a white figure coming rapidly down through the grove, under the flickering leaf shadows,—Mrs. Forrester, bareheaded, a basket on her arm, her blue-black hair shining in the sun. It was not until years afterward that she began to wear veils and sun hats, though her complexion was never one of her beauties. Her cheeks were pale and rather thin, slightly freckled in summer.

As she approached, George Adams, who had a particular mother, rose, and Niel followed his example.

"Here are some hot cookies for your lunch, boys." She took the napkin off the basket. "Did you catch anything?"

"We didn't fish much. Just ran about," said George.

"I know! You were wading and things." She had a nice way of talking to boys, light and confidential. "I wade down there myself sometimes, when I go down to get flowers. I can't resist it. I pull off my stockings and pick up my skirts, and in I go!" She thrust out a white shoe and shook it.

"But you can swim, can't you, Mrs. Forrester," said George. "Most women can't."

"Oh yes, they can! In California everybody swims. But the Sweet Water doesn't tempt me, —mud and water snakes and blood-suckers— Ugh!" she shivered, laughing.

"We seen a water snake this morning and chased him. A whopper!" Thad Grimes put in.

"Why didn't you kill him? Next time I go wading he'll bite my toes! Now, go on with your lunch. George can leave the basket with Mary as you go out." She left them, and they watched her white figure drifting along the edge of the grove as she stopped here and there to examine the raspberry vines by the fence.

"These are good cookies, all right," said one of the giggly brown Weaver twins. The German boys munched in silence. They were all rather pleased that Mrs. Forrester had come down to them herself, instead of sending Mary. Even rough little Thad Grimes, with his red thatch and catfish mouth—the characteristic feature of all the Grimes brood—knew that Mrs. Forrester was a very special kind of person. George and Niel were already old enough to see for themselves that she was different from the other townswomen, and to reflect upon what it was that made her so. The Blum brothers regarded her humbly from under their pale, chewed-off hair, as one of the rich and great of the world. They realized, more than their companions, that such a fortunate and privileged class was an axiomatic fact in the social order.

The boys had finished their lunch and were lying on the grass talking about how Judge Pommeroy's water spaniel, Fanny, had been poisoned, and who had certainly done it, when they had a second visitor.

"Shut up, boys, there he comes now. That's Poison Ivy," said one of the Weaver twins. "Shut up, we don't want old Roger poisoned."

A well-grown boy of eighteen or nineteen, dressed in a shabby corduroy hunting suit, with a gun and gamebag, had climbed up from the marsh and was coming down the grove between the rows of trees. He walked with a rude, arrogant stride, kicking at the twigs, and carried himself with unnatural erectness, as if he had a steel rod down his back. There was something defiant and suspicious about the way he held his head. He came up to the group and addressed them in a superior, patronizing tone.

"Hullo, kids. What are *you* doing here?"

"Picnic," said Ed Elliott.

"I thought girls went on picnics. Did you bring teacher along? Ain't you kids old enough to hunt yet?"

George Adams looked at him scornfully. "Of course we are. I got a 22 Remington for my last birthday. But we know better than to bring guns over here. You better hide yours, Mr. Ivy, or Mrs. Forrester will come down and tell you to get out."

"She can't see us from the house. And anyhow, she can't say anything to me. I'm just as good as she is."

To this the boys made no reply. Such an assertion was absurd even to fish-mouthed Thad; his father's business depended upon some people being better than others, and ordering better cuts of meat in consequence. If everybody ate round steak like Ivy Peters' family, there would be nothing in the butcher's trade.

The visitor had put his gun and gamebag behind a tree, however, and stood stiffly upright, surveying the group out of his narrow beady eyes and making them all uncomfortable. George and Niel hated to look at Ivy,—and yet his face had a kind of fascination for them. It was red, and the flesh looked hard, as if it were swollen from bee-stings, or from an encounter with poison ivy. This nickname, however, was given him because it was well known that he had "made away" with several other dogs before he had poisoned the Judge's friendly water spaniel. The boys said he took a dislike to a dog and couldn't rest until he made an end of him.

Ivy's red skin was flecked with tiny freckles, like rust spots, and in each of his hard cheeks there was a curly indentation, like a knot in a tree-bole,—two permanent dimples which did anything but soften his countenance. His eyes were very small, and an absence of eyelashes gave his pupils the fixed, unblinking hardness of a snake's

or a lizard's. His hands had the same swollen
look as his face, were deeply creased across the
back and knuckles, as if the skin were stretched
too tight. He was an ugly fellow, Ivy Peters,
and he liked being ugly.

He began telling the boys that it was too hot
to hunt now, but later he meant to steal down
to the marsh, where the ducks came at sundown,
and bag a few. "I can make off across the corn
fields before the old Cap sees me. He's not
much on the run."

"He'll complain to your father."

"A whoop my father cares!" The speaker's
restless eyes were looking up through the
branches. "See that woodpecker tapping; don't
mind us a bit. That's nerve!"

"They are protected here, so they're not
afraid," said precise George.

"Hump! They'll spoil the old man's grove
for him. That tree's full of holes already.
Wouldn't he come down easy, now!"

Niel and George Adams sat up. "Don't you
dare shoot here, you'll get us all into trouble."

"She'd come right down from the house," cried
Ed Elliott.

"Let her come, stuck-up piece! Who's talking
about shooting, anyway? There's more ways
of killing dogs than choking them with butter."

At this effrontery the boys shot amazed glances at one another, and the brown Weaver twins broke simultaneously into giggles and rolled over on the turf. But Ivy seemed unaware that he was regarded as being especially resourceful where dogs were concerned. He drew from his pocket a metal sling-shot and some round bits of gravel. "I won't kill it. I'll just surprise it, so we can have a look at it."

"Bet you won't hit it!"

"Bet I will!" He fitted the stone to the leather, squinted, and let fly. Sure enough, the woodpecker dropped at his feet. He threw his heavy black felt hat over it. Ivy never wore a straw hat, even in the hottest weather. "Now wait. He'll come to. You'll hear him flutter in a minute."

"It ain't a he, anyhow. It's a female. Anybody would know that," said Niel contemptuously, annoyed that this unpopular boy should come along and spoil their afternoon. He held the fate of his uncle's spaniel against Ivy Peters.

"All right, Miss Female," said Ivy carelessly, intent upon a project of his own. He took from his pocket a little red leather box, and when he opened it the boys saw that it contained curious little instruments: tiny sharp knife blades, hooks, curved needles, a saw, a blow-pipe, and scissors.

"Some of these I got with a taxidermy outfit from the *Youth's Companion,* and some I made myself." He got stiffly down on his knees,—his joints seemed disinclined to bend at all,—and listened beside his hat. "She's as lively as a cricket," he announced. Thrusting his hand suddenly under the brim, he brought out the startled bird. It was not bleeding, and did not seem to be crippled.

"Now, you watch, and I'll show you something," said Ivy. He held the woodpecker's head in a vice made of his thumb and forefinger, enclosing its panting body with his palm. Quick as a flash, as if it were a practised trick, with one of those tiny blades he slit both the eyes that glared in the bird's stupid little head, and instantly released it.

The woodpecker rose in the air with a whirling, corkscrew motion, darted to the right, struck a tree-trunk,—to the left, and struck another. Up and down, backward and forward among the tangle of branches it flew, raking its feathers, falling and recovering itself. The boys stood watching it, indignant and uncomfortable, not knowing what to do. They were not especially sensitive; Thad was always on hand when there was anything doing at the slaughter house, and the Blum boys lived by killing things. They wouldn't have believed they could be so upset by a hurt woodpecker. There was something wild and desperate about the way the darkened creature beat its wings in the branches, whirling in the sunlight and never seeing it, always thrusting its head up and shaking it, as a bird does when it is drinking. Presently it managed to get its feet on the same limb where it had been struck, and seemed to recognize that perch. As if it had learned something by its bruises, it pecked and crept its way along the branch and disappeared into its own hole.

"There," Niel Herbert exclaimed between his teeth, "if I can get it now, I can kill it and put it out of its misery. Let me on your back, Rhein."

Rheinhold was the tallest, and he obediently bent his bony back. The trunk of a cottonwood tree is hard to climb; the bark is rough, and the branches begin a long way up. Niel tore his trousers and scratched his bare legs smartly before he got to the first fork. After recovering breath, he wound his way up toward the woodpecker's hole, which was inconveniently high. He was almost there, his companions below thought him quite safe, when he suddenly lost his balance, turned a somersault in the air, and bumped down on the grass at their feet. There he lay without moving.

"Run for water!"

"Run for Mrs. Forrester! Ask her for whiskey."

"No," said George Adams, "let's carry him up to the house. She will know what to do."

"That's sense," said Ivy Peters. As he was much bigger and stronger than any of the others, he lifted Niel's limp body and started up the hill. It had occurred to him that this would be a fine chance to get inside the Forresters' house and see what it was like, and this he had always wanted to do.

Mary, the cook, saw them coming from the kitchen window, and ran for her mistress. Captain Forrester was in Kansas City that day.

Mrs. Forrester came to the back door. "What's happened? It's Niel, too! Bring him in this way, please."

Ivy Peters followed her, keeping his eyes open, and the rest trooped after him,—all but the Blum boys, who knew that their place was outside the kitchen door. Mrs. Forrester led the way through the butler's pantry, the dining room, the back parlour, to her own bedroom. She threw down the white counterpane, and Ivy laid Niel upon the sheets. Mrs. Forrester was concerned, but not frightened.

"Mary, will you bring the brandy from the sideboard. George, telephone Dr. Dennison to come over at once. Now you other boys run out on the front porch and wait quietly. There are too many of you in here." She knelt by the bed, putting brandy between Niel's white lips with a teaspoon. The little boys withdrew, only Ivy Peters remained standing in the back parlour, just outside the bedroom door, his arms folded across his chest, taking in his surroundings with bold, unblinking eyes.

Mrs. Forrester glanced at him over her shoulder. "Will you wait on the porch, please? You are older than the others, and if anything is needed I can call on you."

Ivy cursed himself, but he had to go. There was something final about her imperious courtesy,—high-and-mighty, he called it. He had intended to sit down in the biggest leather chair and cross his legs and make himself at home; but he found himself on the front porch, put out by that delicately modulated voice as effectually as if he had been kicked out by the brawniest tough in town.

Niel opened his eyes and looked wonderingly about the big, half-darkened room, full of heavy, old-fashioned walnut furniture. He was lying on a white bed with ruffled pillow shams, and Mrs. Forrester was kneeling beside him, bathing his forehead with cologne. Bohemian Mary stood behind her, with a basin of water. "Ouch, my arm!" he muttered, and the perspiration broke out on his face.

"Yes, dear, I'm afraid it's broken. Don't move. Dr. Dennison will be here in a few minutes. It doesn't hurt very much, does it?"

"No'm," he said faintly. He was in pain, but he felt weak and contented. The room was cool and dusky and quiet. At his house everything was horrid when one was sick. . . . What soft fingers Mrs. Forrester had, and what a lovely lady she was. Inside the lace ruffle of her dress he saw her white throat rising and falling so quickly. Suddenly she got up to take off her glittering rings,—she had not thought of them before,—shed them off her fingers with a quick motion as if she were washing her hands, and dropped them into Mary's broad palm. The little boy was thinking that he would probably never be in so nice a place again. The windows went almost down to the baseboard, like doors, and the closed green shutters let in streaks of sunlight that quivered on the polished floor and the silver things on the dresser. The heavy curtains were looped back with thick cords, like ropes. The marble-topped washstand was as big as a sideboard. The massive walnut furniture was all inlaid with pale-coloured woods. Niel had a scroll-saw, and this inlay interested him.

"There, he looks better now, doesn't he, Mary?" Mrs. Forrester ran her fingers through his black hair and lightly kissed him on the forehead. Oh, how sweet, how sweet she smelled!

"Wheels on the bridge; it's Doctor Dennison. Go and show him in, Mary."

Dr. Dennison set Niel's arm and took him home in his buggy. Home was not a pleasant place to go to; a frail egg-shell house, set off on the edge of the prairie where people of no consequence lived. Except for the fact that he was Judge Pommeroy's nephew, Niel would have been one of the boys to whom Mrs. Forrester merely nodded brightly as she passed. His father was a widower. A poor relation, a spinster from Kentucky, kept house for them, and Niel thought she was probably the worst housekeeper in the world. Their house was usually full of washing in various stages of incompletion,—tubs sitting about with linen soaking,— and the beds were "aired" until any hour in the afternoon when Cousin Sadie happened to think of making them up. She liked to sit down after breakfast and read murder trials, or peruse a well-worn copy of "St. Elmo." Sadie was a good-natured thing and was always running off to help a neighbour, but Niel hated to have anyone come to see them. His father was at home very little, spent all his time at his office. He kept the county abstract books and made farm loans. Having lost his own property, he invested other people's money for them. He was a gentle, agreeable man, young, good-looking, with nice manners, but Niel felt there was an air of failure and defeat about his family. He clung to his maternal uncle, Judge Pommeroy, white-whiskered and portly, who was Captain Forrester's lawyer and a friend of all the great men who visited the Forresters. Niel was proud, like his mother; she died when he was five years old. She had hated the West, and used haughtily to tell her neighbours that she would never think of living anywhere but in Fayette county, Kentucky; that they had only come to Sweet Water to make investments and to "turn the crown into the pound." By that phrase she was still remembered, poor lady.

III

FOR the next few years Niel saw very little of Mrs. Forrester. She was an excitement that came and went with summer. She and her husband always spent the winter in Denver and Colorado Springs,—left Sweet Water soon after Thanksgiving and did not return until the first of May. He knew that Mrs. Forrester liked him, but she hadn't much time for growing boys. When she had friends staying with her, and gave a picnic supper for them, or a dance in the grove on a moonlight night, Niel was always invited. Coming and going along the road to the marsh with the Blum boys, he sometimes met the Captain driving visitors over in the democrat wagon, and he heard about these people from Black Tom, Judge Pommeroy's faithful negro servant, who went over to wait on the table for Mrs. Forrester when she had a dinner party.

Then came the accident which cut short the Captain's career as a roadbuilder. After that fall with his horse, he lay ill at the Antlers, in Colorado Springs, all winter. In the summer, when Mrs. Forrester brought him home to Sweet Water, he still walked with a cane. He had grown much heavier, seemed encumbered by his own bulk, and never suggested taking a contract for the railroad again. He was able to work in his garden, trimmed his snowball bushes and lilac hedges, devoted a great deal of time to growing roses. He and his wife still went away for the winter, but each year the period of their absence grew shorter.

All this while the town of Sweet Water was changing. Its future no longer looked bright. Successive crop failures had broken the spirit of the farmers. George Adams and his family had gone back to Massachusetts, disillusioned about the West. One by one the other gentlemen ranchers followed their example. The Forresters now had fewer visitors. The Burlington was "drawing in its horns," as people said, and the railroad officials were not stopping off at Sweet Water so often,—were more inclined to hurry past a town where they had sunk money that would never come back.

Niel Herbert's father was one of the first failures to be crowded to the wall. He closed his little house, sent his cousin Sadie back to Kentucky, and went to Denver to accept an office position. He left Niel behind to read law in the office with his uncle. Not that Niel had any taste for the law, but he liked being with Judge Pommeroy, and he might as well stay there as anywhere, for the present. The few thousand dollars his mother had left him would not be his until he was twenty-one.

Niel fitted up a room for himself behind the suite which the Judge retained for his law offices, on the second floor of the most pretentious brick block in town. There he lived with monastic cleanliness and severity, glad to be rid of his cousin and her inconsequential housewifery, and resolved to remain a bachelor, like his uncle. He took care of the offices, which meant that he did the janitor work, and arranged them exactly to suit his taste, making the rooms so attractive that all the Judge's friends, and especially Captain Forrester, dropped in there to talk oftener than ever.

The Judge was proud of his nephew. Niel was now nineteen, a tall, straight, deliberate boy. His features were clear-cut, his grey eyes, so dark that they looked black under his long lashes, were rather moody and challenging. The world did not seem over-bright to young people just then. His reserve, which did not come from embarrassment or vanity, but from a critical habit of mind, made him seem older than he was, and a little cold.

One winter afternoon, only a few days before Christmas, Niel sat writing in the back office, at the long table where he usually worked or trifled, surrounded by the Judge's fine law library and solemn steel engravings of statesmen and jurists. His uncle was at his desk in the front office, engaged in a friendly consultation with one of his country clients. Niel, greatly bored with the notes he was copying, was trying to invent an excuse for getting out on the street, when he became aware of light footsteps coming rapidly down the outside corridor. The door of the front office opened, he heard his uncle rise quickly to his feet, and, at the same moment, heard a woman's laugh,—a soft, musical laugh which rose and descended like a suave scale. He turned in his screw chair so that he could look over his shoulder through the double doors into the front room. Mrs. Forrester stood there, shaking her muff at the Judge and the bewildered Swede farmer. Her quick eye lighted upon a bottle of Bourbon and two glasses on the desk among the papers.

"Is that the way you prepare your cases, Judge? What an example for Niel!" She peeped through the door and nodded to the boy as he rose.

He remained in the back room, however, watching her while she declined the chair the Judge pushed toward her and made a sign of refusal when he politely pointed to the Bourbon. She stood beside his desk in her long sealskin coat and cap, a crimson scarf showing above the collar, a little brown veil with spots tied over her eyes. The veil did not in the least obscure those beautiful eyes, dark and full of light, set under a low white forehead and arching eyebrows. The frosty air had brought no colour to her cheeks,—her skin had always the fragrant, crystalline whiteness of white lilacs. Mrs. Forrester looked at one, and one knew that she was bewitching. It was instantaneous, and it pierced the thickest hide. The Swede farmer was now grinning from ear to ear, and he, too, had shuffled to his feet. There could be no negative encounter, however slight, with Mrs. Forrester. If she merely bowed to you, merely looked at you, it constituted a personal relation. Something about her took hold of one in a flash; one became acutely conscious of her, of her fragility and grace, of her mouth which could say so much without words; of her eyes, lively, laughing, intimate, nearly always a little mocking.

"Will you and Niel dine with us tomorrow evening, Judge? And will you lend me Tom? We've just had a wire. The Ogdens are stopping over with us. They've been East to bring the girl home from school,—she's had mumps or something. They want to get home for Christmas, but they will stop off for two days. Probably Frank Ellinger will come on from Denver."

"No prospect can afford me such pleasure as that of dining with Mrs. Forrester," said the Judge ponderously.

"Thank you!" she bowed playfully and turned toward the double doors. "Niel, could you leave your work long enough to drive me home? Mr. Forrester has been detained at the bank."

Niel put on his wolfskin coat. Mrs. Forrester took him by his shaggy sleeve and went with him quickly down the long corridor and the narrow stairs to the street.

At the hitch-bar stood her cutter, looking like a painted toy among the country sleds and wagons. Niel tucked the buffalo robes about Mrs. Forrester, untied the ponies, and sprang in beside her. Without direction the team started down the frozen main street, where few people were abroad, crossed the creek on the ice, and trotted up the poplar-bordered lane toward the house on the hill. The late afternoon sun burned on the snow-crusted pastures. The poplars looked very tall and straight, pinched up and severe in their winter poverty. Mrs. Forrester chatted to Niel with her face turned toward him, holding her muff up to break the wind.

"I'm counting on you to help me entertain Constance Ogden. Can you take her off my hands day after tomorrow, come over in the afternoon? Your duties as a lawyer aren't very arduous yet?" She smiled teasingly. "What can I do with a miss of nineteen? one who goes to college? I've no learned conversation for her!"

"Surely I haven't!" Niel exclaimed.

"Oh, but you're a boy! Perhaps you can interest her in lighter things. She's considered pretty."

"Do you think she is?"

"I haven't seen her lately. She was striking, —china blue eyes and heaps of yellow hair, not exactly yellow,—what they call an ashen blond, I believe."

Niel had noticed that in describing the charms of other women Mrs. Forrester always made fun of them a little.

They drew up in front of the house. Ben Keezer came round from the kitchen to take the team.

"You are to go back for Mr. Forrester at six, Ben. Niel, come in for a moment and get warm." She drew him through the little storm entry, which protected the front door in winter, into the hall. "Hang up your coat and come along." He followed her through the parlour into the sitting-room, where a little coal grate was burning under the black mantelpiece, and sat down in the big leather chair in which Captain Forrester dozed after his mid-day meal. It was a rather dark room, with walnut bookcases that had carved tops and glass doors. The floor was covered by a red carpet, and the walls were hung with large, old-fashioned engravings; "The House of the Poet on the Last Day of Pompeii," "Shakespeare Reading before Queen Elizabeth."

Mrs. Forrester left him and presently returned carrying a tray with a decanter and sherry glasses. She put it down on her husband's smoking-table, poured out a glass for Niel and one for herself, and perched on the arm of one of the stuffed chairs, where she sat sipping her sherry and stretching her tiny, silver-buckled slippers out toward the glowing coals.

"It's so nice to have you staying on until after Christmas," Niel observed. "You've only been here one other Christmas since I can remember."

"I'm afraid we're staying on all winter this year. Mr. Forrester thinks we can't afford to go away. For some reason, we are extraordinarily poor just now."

"Like everybody else," the boy commented grimly

"Yes, like everybody else. However, it does no good to be glum about it, does it?" She refilled the two glasses. "I always take a little sherry at this time in the afternoon. At Colorado Springs some of my friends take tea, like the English. But I should feel like an old woman, drinking tea! Besides, sherry is good for my throat." Niel remembered some legend about a weak chest and occasional terrifying hemorrhages. But that seemed doubtful, as one looked at her,—fragile, indeed, but with such light, effervescing vitality. "Perhaps I do seem old to you, Niel, quite old enough for tea and a cap!"

He smiled gravely. "You seem always the same to me, Mrs. Forrester."

"Yes? And how is that?"

"Lovely. Just lovely."

As she bent forward to put down her glass she patted his cheek. "Oh, you'll do very well for Constance!" Then, seriously, "I'm glad if I do, though. I want you to like me well enough to come to see us often this winter. You shall come with your uncle to make a fourth at whist. Mr. Forrester must have his whist in the evening. Do you think he is looking any worse, Niel? It frightens me to see him getting a little uncertain. But there, we must believe in good luck!" She took up the half-empty glass and held it against the light.

Niel liked to see the firelight sparkle on her earrings, long pendants of garnets and seed-pearls in the shape of fleurs-de-lys. She was the only woman he knew who wore earrings; they hung naturally against her thin, triangular cheeks. Captain Forrester, although he had given her handsomer ones, liked to see her wear these, because they had been his mother's. It gratified him to have his wife wear jewels; it meant something to him. She never left off her beautiful rings unless she was in the kitchen.

"A winter in the country may do him good," said Mrs. Forrester, after a silence during which she looked intently into the fire, as if she were trying to read the outcome of their difficulties there. "He loves this place so much. But you and Judge Pommeroy must keep an eye on him when he is in town, Niel. If he looks tired or uncertain, make some excuse and bring him home. He can't carry a drink or two as he used,"—she glanced over her shoulder to see that the door into the dining-room was shut. "Once last winter he had been drinking with some old friends at the Antlers,—nothing unusual, just as he always did, as a man must be able to do,—but it was too much for him. When he came out to join me in the carriage, coming down that long walk, you know, he fell. There was no ice, he didn't slip. It was simply because he was unsteady. He had trouble getting up. I still shiver to think of it. To me, it was as if one of the mountains had fallen down."

A little later Niel went plunging down the hill, looking exultantly into the streak of red sunset. Oh, the winter would not be so bad, this year! How strange that she should be here at all, a woman like her among common people! Not even in Denver had he ever seen another woman so elegant. He had sat in the dining-room of the Brown Palace hotel and watched them as they came down to dinner,—fashionable women from "the East," on their way to California. But he had never found one so attractive and distinguished as Mrs. Forrester. Compared with her, other women were heavy and dull; even the pretty ones seemed lifeless,—they had not that something in their glance that made one's blood tingle. And never elsewhere had he heard anything like her inviting, musical laugh, that was like the distant measures of dance music, heard through opening and shutting doors.

He could remember the very first time he ever saw Mrs. Forrester, when he was a little boy. He had been loitering in front of the Episcopal church one Sunday morning, when a low carriage drove up to the door. Ben Keezer was on the front seat, and on the back seat was a lady, alone, in a black silk dress all puffs and ruffles, and a black hat, carrying a parasol with a carved ivory handle. As the carriage stopped she lifted her dress to alight; out of a swirl of foamy white petticoats she thrust a black, shiny slipper. She stepped lightly to the ground and with a nod to the driver went into the church. The little boy followed her through the open door, saw her enter a pew and kneel. He was proud now that at the first moment he had recognized her as belonging to a different world from any he had ever known.

Niel paused for a moment at the end of the lane to look up at the last skeleton poplar in the long row; just above its pointed tip hung the hollow, silver winter moon.

IV

IN pleasant weather Judge Pommeroy walked
to the Forresters', but on the occasion of
the dinner for the Ogdens he engaged the
liveryman to take him and his nephew over in
one of the town hacks,—vehicles seldom used except for funerals and weddings. They smelled
strongly of the stable and contained lap-robes as
heavy as lead and as slippery as oiled paper.
Niel and his uncle were the only townspeople
asked to the Forresters' that evening; they rolled
over the creek and up the hill in state, and
emerged covered with horsehair.

Captain Forrester met them at the door, his
burly figure buttoned up in a frock coat, a flat
collar and black string tie under the heavy folds
of his neck. He was always clean-shaven except
for a drooping dun-coloured moustache. The
company stood behind him laughing while Niel
caught up the whisk-broom and began dusting
roan hairs off his uncle's broadcloth. Mrs. Forrester gave Niel a brushing in turn and then took
him into the parlour and introduced him to Mrs.
Ogden and her daughter.

The daughter was a rather pretty girl, Niel thought, in a pale pink evening dress which left bare her smooth arms and short, dimpled neck. Her eyes were, as Mrs. Forrester had said, a china blue, rather prominent and inexpressive. Her fleece of ashy-gold hair was bound about her head with silver bands. In spite of her fresh, rose-like complexion, her face was not altogether agreeable. Two dissatisfied lines reached from the corners of her short nose to the corners of her mouth. When she was displeased, even a little, these lines tightened, drew her nose back, and gave her a suspicious, injured expression. Niel sat down by her and did his best, but he found her hard to talk to. She seemed nervous and distracted, kept glancing over her shoulder, and crushing her handkerchief up in her hands. Her mind, clearly, was elsewhere. After a few moments he turned to the mother, who was more easily interested.

Mrs. Ogden was almost unpardonably homely. She had a pear-shaped face, and across her high forehead lay a row of flat, dry curls. Her bluish brown skin was almost the colour of her violet dinner dress. A diamond necklace glittered about her wrinkled throat. Unlike Constance, she seemed thoroughly amiable, but as she talked she tilted her head and "used" her eyes, availing herself of those arch glances which he had supposed only pretty women indulged in. Probably she had long been surrounded by people to whom she was an important personage, and had acquired the manner of a spoiled darling. Niel thought her rather foolish at first, but in a few moments he had got used to her mannerisms and began to like her. He found himself laughing heartily and forgot the discouragement of his failure with the daughter.

Mr. Ogden, a short, weather-beaten man of fifty, with a cast in one eye, a stiff imperial, and twisted moustaches, was noticeably quieter and less expansive than when Niel had met him here on former occasions. He seemed to expect his wife to do the talking. When Mrs. Forrester addressed him, or passed near him, his good eye twinkled and followed her,—while the eye that looked askance remained unchanged and committed itself to nothing.

Suddenly everyone became more lively; the air warmed, and the lamplight seemed to brighten, as a fourth member of the Denver party came in from the dining-room with a glittering tray full of cocktails he had been making. Frank Ellinger was a bachelor of forty, six feet two, with long straight legs, fine shoulders, and a figure that still permitted his white waistcoat to button without a wrinkle under his conspicuously well-cut dinner coat. His black hair, coarse and curly as the filling of a mattress, was grey about the ears, his florid face showed little purple veins about his beaked nose,—a nose like the prow of a ship, with long nostrils. His chin was deeply cleft, his thick curly lips seemed very muscular, very much under his control, and, with his strong white teeth, irregular and curved, gave him the look of a man who could bite an iron rod in two with a snap of his jaws. His whole figure seemed very much alive under his clothes, with a restless, muscular energy that had something of the cruelty of wild animals in it. Niel was very much interested in this man, the hero of many ambiguous stories. He didn't know whether he liked him or not. He knew nothing bad about him, but he felt something evil.

The cocktails were the signal for general conversation, the company drew together in one group. Even Miss Constance seemed less dissatisfied. Ellinger drank his cocktail standing beside her chair, and offered her the cherry in his glass. They were old-fashioned whiskey cocktails. Nobody drank Martinis then; gin was supposed to be the consolation of sailors and inebriate scrub-women.

"Very good, Frank, very good," Captain Forrester pronounced, drawing out a fresh, cologne-scented handkerchief to wipe his moustache. "Are encores in order?" The Captain puffed slightly when he talked. His eyes, always somewhat suffused and bloodshot since his injury, blinked at his friends from under his heavy lids.

"One more round for everybody, Captain." Ellinger brought in from the sideboard a capacious shaker and refilled all the glasses except Miss Ogden's. At her he shook his finger, and offered her the little dish of Maraschino cherries.

"No, I don't want those. I want the one in your glass," she said with a pouty smile. "I like it to taste of something!"

"Constance!" said her mother reprovingly, rolling her eyes at Mrs. Forrester, as if to share with her the charm of such innocence.

"Niel," Mrs. Forrester laughed, "won't you give the child your cherry, too?"

Niel promptly crossed the room and proffered the cherry in the bottom of his glass. She took it with her thumb and fore-finger and dropped it into her own,—where, he was quick to observe, she left it when they went out to dinner. A stubborn piece of pink flesh, he decided, and certainly a fool about a man quite old enough to be her father. He sighed when he saw that he was placed next her at the dinner table.

Captain Forrester still made a commanding figure at the head of his own table, with his napkin tucked under his chin and the work of carving well in hand. Nobody could lay bare the bones of a brace of duck or a twenty-pound turkey more deftly. "What part of the turkey do you prefer, Mrs. Ogden?" If one had a preference, it was gratified, with all the stuffing and gravy that went with it, and the vegetables properly placed. When a plate left Captain Forrester's hands, it was a dinner; the recipient was served, and well served. He served Mrs. Forrester last of the ladies but before the men, and to her, too, he said, "Mrs. Forrester, what part of the turkey shall I give you this evening?" He was a man who did not vary his formulae or his manners. He was no more mobile than his countenance. Niel and Judge Pommeroy had often remarked how much Captain Forrester looked like the pictures of Grover Cleveland. His clumsy dignity covered a deep nature, and a conscience that had never been juggled with. His repose was like that of a mountain. When he laid his fleshy, thick-fingered hand upon a frantic horse, an hysterical woman, an Irish workman out for blood, he brought them peace; something they could not resist. That had been the secret of his management of men. His sanity asked nothing, claimed nothing; it was so simple that it brought a hush over distracted creatures. In the old days, when he was building road in the Black Hills. trouble sometimes broke out in camp when he was absent, staying with Mrs. Forrester at Colorado Springs. He would put down the telegram that announced an insurrection and say to his wife, "Maidy, I must go to the men." And that was all he did,—he went to them.

While the Captain was intent upon his duties as host he talked very little, and Judge Pommeroy and Ellinger kept a lively cross-fire of amusing stories going. Niel, sitting opposite Ellinger, watched him closely. He still couldn't decide whether he liked him or not. In Denver Frank was known as a prince of good fellows; tactful, generous, resourceful, though apt to trim his sails to the wind; a man who good-humouredly bowed to the inevitable, or to the almost-inevitable. He had, when he was younger, been notoriously "wild," but that was not held against him, even by mothers with marriageable daughters, like Mrs. Ogden. Morals were different in those days. Niel had heard his uncle refer to Ellinger's youthful infatuation with a woman

called Nell Emerald, a handsome and rather unusual woman who conducted a house properly
licensed by the Denver police. Nell Emerald
had told an old club man that though she had
been out behind young Ellinger's new trotting
horse, she "had no respect for a man who would
go driving with a prostitute in broad daylight."
This story and a dozen like it were often related
of Ellinger, and the women laughed over them
as heartily as the men. All the while that he was
making a scandalous chronicle for himself, young
Ellinger had been devotedly caring for an invalid
mother, and he was described to strangers as
a terribly fast young man and a model son. That
combination pleased the taste of the time. Nobody thought the worse of him. Now that his
mother was dead, he lived at the Brown Palace
hotel, though he still kept her house at Colorado
Springs.

When the roast was well under way, Black
Tom, very formal in a white waistcoat and high
collar, poured the champagne. Captain Forrester lifted his glass, the frail stem between his
thick fingers, and glancing round the table at his
guests and at Mrs. Forrester, said,

"Happy days!"

It was the toast he always drank at dinner, the
invocation he was sure to utter when he took a

glass of whiskey with an old friend. Whoever had heard him say it once, liked to hear him say it again. Nobody else could utter those two words as he did, with such gravity and high courtesy. It seemed a solemn moment, seemed to knock at the door of Fate; behind which all days, happy and otherwise, were hidden. Niel drank his wine with a pleasant shiver, thinking that nothing else made life seem so precarious, the future so cryptic and unfathomable, as that brief toast uttered by the massive man, "Happy days!"

Mrs. Ogden turned to the host with her most languishing smile: "Captain Forrester, I want you to tell Constance"— (She was an East Virginia woman, and what she really said was, "Cap'n Forrester, Ah wan' yew to tell, etc." Her vowels seemed to roll about in the same way her eyes did.)—"I want you to tell Constance about how you first found this lovely spot, 'way back in Indian times."

The Captain looked down the table between the candles at Mrs. Forrester, as if to consult her. She smiled and nodded, and her beautiful earrings swung beside her pale cheeks. She was wearing her diamonds tonight, and a black velvet gown. Her husband had archaic ideas about jewels; a man bought them for his wife in acknowledgment of things he could not gracefully utter. They must be costly; they must show that he was able to buy them, and that she was worthy to wear them.

With her approval the Captain began his narrative: a concise account of how he came West a young boy, after serving in the Civil War, and took a job as driver for a freighting company that carried supplies across the plains from Nebraska City to Cherry Creek, as Denver was then called. The freighters, after embarking in that sea of grass six hundred miles in width, lost all count of the days of the week and the month. One day was like another, and all were glorious; good hunting, plenty of antelope and buffalo, boundless sunny sky, boundless plains of waving grass, long fresh-water lagoons yellow with lagoon flowers, where the bison in their periodic migrations stopped to drink and bathe and wallow.

"An ideal life for a young man," the Captain pronounced. Once, when he was driven out of the trail by a wash-out, he rode south on his horse to explore, and found an Indian encampment near the Sweet Water, on this very hill where his house now stood. He was, he said, "greatly taken with the location," and made up his mind that he would one day have a house there. He cut down a young willow tree and drove the stake into the ground to mark the spot where he wished to build. He went away and did not come back for many years; he was helping to lay the first railroad across the plains.

"There were those that were dependent on me," he said. "I had sickness to contend with, and responsibilities. But in all those years I expect there was hardly a day passed that I did not remember the Sweet Water and this hill. When I came here a young man, I had planned it in my mind, pretty much as it is today; where I would dig my well, and where I would plant my grove and my orchard. I planned to build a house that my friends could come to, with a wife like Mrs. Forrester to make it attractive to them. I used to promise myself that some day I would manage it." This part of the story the Captain told not with embarrassment, but with reserve, choosing his words slowly, absently cracking English walnuts with his strong fingers and heaping a little hoard of kernels beside his plate. His friends understood that he was referring to his first marriage, to the poor invalid wife who had never been happy and who had kept his nose to the grindstone.

"When things looked most discouraging," he went on, "I came back here once and bought the place from the railroad company. They took my note. I found my willow stake,—it had rooted and grown into a tree,—and I planted three more to mark the corners of my house. Twelve years later Mrs. Forrester came here with me, shortly after our marriage, and we built our house." Captain Forrester puffed from time to time, but his clear account commanded attention. Something in the way he uttered his unornamented phrases gave them the impressiveness of inscriptions cut in stone.

Mrs. Forrester nodded at him from her end of the table. "And now, tell us your philosophy of life,—this is where it comes in," she laughed teasingly.

The Captain coughed and looked abashed. "I was intending to omit that tonight. Some of our guests have already heard it."

"No, no. It belongs at the end of the story, and if some of us have heard it, we can hear it again. Go on!"

"Well, then, my philosophy is that what you think of and plan for day by day, in spite of yourself, so to speak—you will get. You will get it more or less. That is, unless you are one of the people who get nothing in this world. There are such people. I have lived too much in mining works and construction camps not to know that." He paused as if, though this was too dark a chapter to be gone into, it must have its place, its moment of silent recognition. "If you are not one of those, Constance and Niel, you will accomplish what you dream of most."

"And why? That's the interesting part of it," his wife prompted him.

"Because," he roused himself from his abstraction and looked about at the company, "because a thing that is dreamed of in the way I mean, is already an accomplished fact. All our great West has been developed from such dreams; the homesteader's and the prospector's and the contractor's. We dreamed the railroads across the mountains, just as I dreamed my place on the Sweet Water. All these things will be everyday facts to the coming generation, but to us—" Captain Forrester ended with a sort of grunt. Something forbidding had come into his voice, the lonely, defiant note that is so often heard in the voices of old Indians.

Mrs. Ogden had listened to the story with such sympathy that Niel liked her better than ever, and even the preoccupied Constance seemed able to give it her attention. They rose from the dessert and went into the parlour to arrange the card tables. The Captain still played whist as well as ever. As he brought out a box of his best cigars, he paused before Mrs. Ogden and said, "Is smoke offensive to you, Mrs. Ogden?" When she protested that it was not, he crossed the room to where Constance was talking with Ellinger and asked with the same grave courtesy, "Is smoke offensive to you, Constance?" Had there been half a dozen women present, he would have asked that question of each, probably, and in the same words. It did not bother him to repeat a phrase. If an expression answered his purpose, he saw no reason for varying it.

Mrs. Forrester and Mr. Ogden were to play against Mrs. Ogden and the Captain. "Constance," said Mrs. Forrester as she sat down, "will you play with Niel? I'm told he's very good."

Miss Ogden's short nose flickered up, the lines on either side of it deepened, and she again looked injured. Niel was sure she detested him. He was not going to be done in by her.

"Miss Ogden," he said as he stood beside his chair, deliberately shuffling a pack of cards, "my uncle and I are used to playing together, and probably you are used to playing with Mr. Ellinger. Suppose we try that combination?"

She gave him a quick, suspicious glance from under her yellow eyelashes and flung herself into a chair without so much as answering him. Frank Ellinger came in from the dining-room, where he had been sampling the Captain's French brandy, and took the vacant seat opposite Miss Ogden. "So it's you and me, Connie? Good enough!" he exclaimed, cutting the pack Niel pushed toward him.

Just before midnight Black Tom opened the door and announced that the egg-nog was ready. The card players went into the dining-room, where the punch-bowl stood smoking on the table.

"Constance," said Captain Forrester, "do you sing? I like to hear one of the old songs with the egg-nog."

"Ah'm sorry, Cap'n Forrester. Ah really haven't any voice."

Niel noticed that whenever Constance spoke to the Captain she strained her throat, though he wasn't in the least deaf. He broke in over her refusal. "Uncle can start a song if you coax him, sir."

Judge Pommeroy, after smoothing his silver whiskers and coughing, began "Auld Lang Syne." The others joined in, but they hadn't got to the end of it when a hollow rumbling down on the bridge made them laugh, and everyone ran to the front windows to see the Judge's funeral coach come lurching up the hill, with only one of the side lanterns lit. Mrs. Forrester sent Tom out with a drink for the driver. While Niel and his uncle were putting on their overcoats in the hall, she came up to them and whispered coaxingly to the boy, "Remember, you are coming over tomorrow, at two? I am planning a drive, and I want you to amuse Constance for me."

Niel bit his lip and looked down into Mrs. Forrester's laughing, persuasive eyes. "I'll do it for you, but that's the only reason," he said threateningly.

"I understand, for me! I'll credit it to your account."

The Judge and his nephew rolled away on swaying springs. The Ogdens retired to their rooms upstairs. Mrs. Forrester went to help the Captain divest himself of his frock coat, and put it away for him. Ever since he was hurt he had to be propped high on pillows at night, and he slept in a narrow iron bed, in the alcove which had formerly been his wife's dressing-room. While he was undressing he breathed heavily and sighed, as if he were very tired. He fumbled with his studs, then blew on his fingers and tried again. His wife came to his aid and quickly unbuttoned everything. He did not thank her in words, but submitted grate-fully.

When the iron bed creaked at receiving his

heavy figure, she called from the big bedroom, "Good-night, Mr. Forrester," and drew the heavy curtains that shut off the alcove. She took off her rings and earrings and was beginning to unfasten her black velvet bodice when, at a tinkle of glass from without, she stopped short. Rehooking the shoulder of her gown, she went to the dining-room, now faintly lit by the coal fire in the back parlour. Frank Ellinger was standing at the sideboard, taking a nightcap. The Forrester French brandy was old, and heavy like a cordial.

"Be careful," she murmured as she approached him, "I have a distinct impression that there is some one on the enclosed stairway. There is a wide crack in the door. Ah, but kittens have claws, these days! Pour me just a little. Thank you. I'll have mine in by the fire."

He followed her into the next room, where she stood by the grate, looking at him in the light of the pale blue flames that ran over the fresh coal, put on to keep the fire.

"You've had a good many brandies, Frank," she said, studying his flushed, masterful face.

"Not too many. I'll need them . . . to-night," he replied meaningly.

She nervously brushed back a lock of hair that

had come down a little. "It's not to-night. It's morning. Go to bed and sleep as late as you please. Take care, I heard silk stockings on the stairs. Good-night." She put her hand on the sleeve of his coat; the white fingers clung to the black cloth as bits of paper cling to magnetized iron. Her touch, soft as it was, went through the man, all the feet and inches of him. His broad shoulders lifted on a deep breath. He looked down at her.

Her eyes fell. "Good-night," she said faintly. As she turned quickly away, the train of her velvet dress caught the leg of his broadcloth trousers and dragged with a friction that crackled and threw sparks. Both started. They stood looking at each other for a moment before she actually slipped through the door. Ellinger remained by the hearth, his arms folded tight over his chest, his curly lips compressed, frowning into the fire.

V

NIEL went up the hill the next afternoon, just as the cutter with the two black ponies jingled round the driveway and stopped at the front door. Mrs. Forrester came out on the porch, dressed for a sleigh ride. Ellinger followed her, buttoned up in a long fur-lined coat, showily befrogged down the front, with a glossy astrachan collar. He looked even more powerful and bursting with vigour than last night. His highly-coloured, well-visored countenance shone with a good opinion of himself and of the world.

Mrs. Forrester called to Niel gaily. "We are going down to the Sweet Water to cut cedar boughs for Christmas. Will you keep Constance company? She seems a trifle disappointed at being left behind, but we can't take the big sleigh,—the pole is broken. Be nice to her, there's a good boy!" She pressed his hand, gave him a meaning, confidential smile, and stepped into the sleigh. Ellinger sprang in beside her, and they glided down the hill with a merry tinkle of sleighbells.

Niel found Miss Ogden in the back parlour.

playing solitaire by the fire. She was clearly out
of humour.

"Come in, Mr. Herbert. I think they might
have taken us along, don't you? I want to see
the river my own self. I hate bein' shut up in the
house!"

"Let's go out, then. Wouldn't you like to see
the town?"

Constance seemed not to hear him. She was
wrinkling and unwrinkling her short nose, and
the restless lines about her mouth were fluttering.
"What's to hinder us from getting a sleigh at the
livery barn and going down to the Sweet Water?
I don't suppose the river's private property?"
She gave a nervous, angry laugh and looked
hopefully at Niel.

"We couldn't get anything at this hour. The
livery teams are all out," he said with firmness.

Constance glanced at him suspiciously, then
sat down at the card table and leaned over it,
drawing her plump shoulders together. Her
fluffy yellow hair was wound round her head like
a scarf and held in place by narrow bands of
black velvet.

The ponies had crossed the second creek and
were trotting down the high road toward the
river. Mrs. Forrester expressed her feelings

in a laugh full of mischief. "Is she running after us? Where did she get the idea that she was to come? What a relief to get away!" She lifted her chin and sniffed the air. The day was grey, without sun, and the air was still and dry, a warm cold. "Poor Mr. Ogden," she went on, "how much livelier he is without his ladies! They almost extinguish him. Now aren't you glad you never married?"

"I'm certainly glad I never married a homely woman. What does a man do it for, anyway? She had no money,—and he's always had it, or been on the way to it."

"Well, they're off tomorrow. And Connie! You've reduced her to a state of imbecility, really! What an afternoon Niel must be having!" She laughed as if the idea of his predicament delighted her.

"Who's this kid, anyway?" Ellinger asked her to take the reins for a moment while he drew a cigar from his pocket. "He's a trifle stiff. Does he make himself useful?"

"Oh, he's a nice boy, stranded here like the rest of us. I'm going to train him to be very useful. He's devoted to Mr. Forrester. Handsome, don't you think?"

"So-so." They turned into a by-road that wound along the Sweet Water. Ellinger held the ponies in a little and turned down his high astrachan collar. "Let's have a look at you, Marian."

Mrs. Forrester was holding her muff before her face, to catch the flying particles of snow the ponies kicked up. From behind it she glanced at him sidewise. "Well?" she said teasingly.

He put his arm through hers and settled himself low in the sleigh. "You ought to look at me better than that. It's been a devil of a long while since I've seen you."

"Perhaps it's been too long," she murmured. The mocking spark in her eyes softened perceptibly under the long pressure of his arm. "Yes, it's been long," she admitted lightly.

"You didn't answer the letter I wrote you on the eleventh."

"Didn't I? Well, at any rate I answered your telegram." She drew her head away as his face came nearer. "You'll really have to watch the ponies, my dear, or they'll tumble us out in the snow."

"I don't care. I wish they would!" he said between his teeth. "Why didn't you answer my letter?"

"Oh, I don't remember! You don't write so many."

"It's no satisfaction. You won't let me write you love letters. You say it's risky."

"So it is, and foolish. But now you needn't be so careful. Not too careful!" she laughed softly. "When I'm off in the country for a whole winter, alone, and growing older, I like to   ." she put her hand on his, "to be reminded of pleasanter things."

Ellinger took off his glove with his teeth. His eyes, sweeping the winding road and the low, snow-covered bluffs, had something wolfish in them.

"Be careful, Frank. My rings! You hurt me!"

"Then why didn't you take them off? You used to. Are these your cedars, shall we stop here?"

"No, not here." She spoke very low. "The best ones are farther on, in a deep ravine that winds back into the hills."

Ellinger glanced at her averted head, and his heavy lips twitched in a smile at one corner. The quality of her voice had changed, and he knew the change. They went spinning along the curves of the winding road, saying not a word. Mrs. Forrester sat with her head bent forward, her face half hidden in her muff. At last she told him to stop. To the right of the road he saw a thicket. Behind it a dry watercourse wound into the bluffs. The tops of the dark, still cedars, just visible from the road, indicated its windings.

"Sit still," he said, "while I take out the horses."

When the blue shadows of approaching dusk were beginning to fall over the snow, one of the Blum boys, slipping quietly along through the timber in search of rabbits, came upon the empty cutter standing in the brush, and near it the two ponies, stamping impatiently where they were tied. Adolph slid back into the thicket and lay down behind a fallen log to see what would happen. Not much ever happened to him but weather.

Presently he heard low voices, coming nearer from the ravine. The big stranger who was visiting at the Forresters' emerged, carrying the buffalo robes on one arm; Mrs. Forrester herself was clinging to the other. They walked slowly, wholly absorbed by what they were saying to each other. When they came up to the sleigh, the man spread the robes on the seat and put his hands under Mrs. Forrester's arms to lift her in. But he did not lift her; he stood for a long while holding her crushed up against his breast, her face hidden in his black overcoat.

"What about those damned cedar boughs?" he asked, after he had put her in and covered her up. "Shall I go back and cut some?"

"It doesn't matter," she murmured.

He reached under the seat for a hatchet and went back to the ravine. Mrs. Forrester sat with her eyes closed, her cheek pillowed on her muff, a faint, soft smile on her lips. The air was still and blue; the Blum boy could almost hear her breathe. When the strokes of the hatchet rang out from the ravine, he could see her eyelids flutter . . . soft shivers went through her body.

The man came back and threw the evergreens into the sleigh. When he got in beside her, she slipped her hand through his arm and settled softly against him. "Drive slowly," she murmured, as if she were talking in her sleep. "It doesn't matter if we are late for dinner. Nothing matters." The ponies trotted off.

The pale Blum boy rose from behind his log and followed the tracks up the ravine. When the orange moon rose over the bluffs, he was still sitting under the cedars, his gun on his knee. While Mrs. Forrester had been waiting there in the sleigh, with her eyes closed, feeling so safe,

he could almost have touched her with his hand.
He had never seen her before when her mocking
eyes and lively manner were not between her and
all the world.   If it had been Thad Grimes who
lay behind that log, now, or Ivy Peters?

But with Adolph Blum her secrets were safe.
His mind was feudal; the rich and fortunate
were also the privileged.   These warm-blooded,
quick-breathing people took chances,—followed
impulses only dimly understandable to a boy who
was wet and weather-chapped all the year; who
waded in the mud fishing for cat, or lay in the
marsh waiting for wild duck.   Mrs. Forrester
had never been too haughty to smile at him
when he came to the back door with his fish.
She never haggled about the price.   She treated
him like a human being.   His little chats with
her, her nod and smile when she passed him on
the street, were among the pleasantest things he
had to remember.   She bought game of him in
the closed season, and didn't give him away.

VI

IT was during that winter, the first one Mrs. Forrester had ever spent in the house on the hill, that Niel came to know her very well. For the Forresters that winter was a sort of isthmus between two estates; soon afterward came a change in their fortunes. And for Niel it was a natural turning-point, since in the autumn he was nineteen, and in the spring he was twenty,—a very great difference.

After the Christmas festivities were over, the whist parties settled into a regular routine. Three evenings a week Judge Pommeroy and his nephew sat down to cards with the Forresters. Sometimes they went over early and dined there. Sometimes they stayed for a late supper after the last rubber. Niel, who had been so content with a bachelor's life, and who had made up his mind that he would never live in a place that was under the control of women, found himself becoming attached to the comforts of a well-conducted house; to the pleasures of the table, to the soft chairs and soft lights and agreeable human voices at the Forresters'. On bitter, windy nights, sitting in his favourite blue chair before the grate, he used to wonder how he could manage to tear himself away, to plunge into the outer darkness, and run down the long frozen road and up the dead street of the town. Captain Forrester was experimenting with bulbs that winter, and had built a little glass conservatory on the south side of the house, off the back parlour. Through January and February the house was full of narcissus and Roman hyacinths, and their heavy, spring-like odour made a part of the enticing comfort of the fireside there.

Where Mrs. Forrester was, dulness was impossible, Niel believed. The charm of her conversation was not so much in what she said, though she was often witty, but in the quick recognition of her eyes, in the living quality of her voice itself. One could talk with her about the most trivial things, and go away with a high sense of elation. The secret of it, he supposed, was that she couldn't help being interested in people, even very commonplace people. If Mr. Ogden or Mr. Dalzell were not there to tell their best stories for her, then she could be amused by Ivy Peters' ruffianly manners, or the soft compliments of old man Elliott when he sold her a pair of winter shoes. She had a fascinating gift of mimicry. When she mentioned the fat iceman, or Thad Grimes at his meat block, or the Blum boys with their dead rabbits, by a subtle suggestion of their manner she made them seem more individual and vivid than they were in their own person. She often caricatured people to their faces, and they were not offended, but greatly flattered. Nothing pleased one more than to provoke her laughter. Then you felt you were getting on with her. It was her form of commenting, of agreeing with you and appreciating you when you said something interesting,—and it often told you a great deal that was both too direct and too elusive for words.

Long, long afterward, when Niel did not know whether Mrs. Forrester were living or dead, if her image flashed into his mind, it came with a brightness of dark eyes, her pale triangular cheeks with long earrings, and her many-coloured laugh. When he was dull, dull and tired of everything, he used to think that if he could hear that long-lost lady laugh again, he could be gay.

The big storm of the winter came late that year; swept down over Sweet Water the first day of March and beat upon the town for three days and nights. Thirty inches of snow fell, and the cutting wind blew it into whirling drifts. The Forresters were snowed in. Ben Keezer, their man of all work, did not attempt to break a road or even to come over to the town himself. On the third day Niel went to the post-office, got the Captain's leather mail sack with its accumulation of letters, and set off across the creek, plunging into drifts up to his middle, sometimes up to his arm-pits. The fences along the lane were covered, but he broke his trail by keeping between the two lines of poplars. When at last he reached the front porch, Captain Forrester came to the door and let him in.

"Glad to see you, my boy, very glad. It's been a little lonesome for us. You must have had hard work getting over. I certainly appreciate it. Come to the sitting-room fire and dry yourself. We will talk quietly. Mrs. Forrester has gone upstairs to lie down; she's been complaining of a headache."

Niel stood before the fire in his rubber boots, drying his trousers. The Captain did not sit down but opened the glass door into his little conservatory.

"I've something pretty to show you, Niel. All my hyacinths are coming along at once, every colour of the rainbow. The Roman hyacinths, I say, are Mrs. Forrester's. They seem to suit her."

Niel went to the door and looked with keen

—72—

pleasure at the fresh, watery blossoms. "I was afraid you might lose them this bitter weather, Captain."

"No, these things can stand a good deal of cold. They've been company for us." He stood looking out through the glass at the drifted shrubbery. Niel liked to see him look out over his place. A man's house is his castle, his look seemed to say. "Ben tells me the rabbits have come up to the barn to eat the hay, everything green is covered up. I had him throw a few cabbages out for them, so they won't suffer. Mrs. Forrester has been on the porch every day, feeding the snow birds," he went on, as if talking to himself.

The stair door opened, and Mrs. Forrester came down in her Japanese dressing-gown, looking very pale. The dark shadows under her eyes seemed to mean that she had been losing sleep.

"Oh, it's Niel! How nice of you. And you've brought the mail. Are there any letters for me?"

"Three. Two from Denver and one from California." Her husband gave them to her. "Did you sleep, Maidy?"

"No, but I rested. It's delightful up in the west room, the wind sings and whistles about the eaves. If you'll excuse me, I'll dress and glance at my letters. Stand closer to the fire, Niel. Are you very wet?" When she stopped beside him to feel his clothes, he smelled a sharp odour of spirits. Was she ill, he wondered, or merely so bored that she had been trying to dull herself?

When she came back she had dressed and re-arranged her hair.

"Mrs. Forrester," said the Captain in a solicitous tone, "I believe I would like some tea and toast this afternoon, like your English friends, and it would be good for your head. We won't offer Niel anything else."

"Very well. Mary has gone to bed with a toothache, but I will make the tea. Niel can make the toast here by the fire while you read your paper."

She was cheerful now,—tied one of Mary's aprons about Niel's neck and set him down with the toasting fork. He noticed that the Captain, as he read his paper, kept his eye on the sideboard with a certain watchfulness, and when his wife brought the tray with tea, and no sherry, he seemed very much pleased. He drank three cups, and took a second piece of toast.

"You see, Mr. Forrester," she said lightly, "Niel has brought back my appetite. I ate no lunch to-day," turning to the boy, "I've been shut up too long. Is there anything in the papers?"

This meant was there any news concerning the people they knew. The Captain put on his silver-rimmed glasses again and read aloud about the doings of their friends in Denver and Omaha and Kansas City. Mrs. Forrester sat on a stool by the fire, eating toast and making humorous comments upon the subjects of those solemn paragraphs; the engagement of Miss Erma Salton-Smith, etc.

"At last, thank God! You remember her, Niel. She's been here. I think you danced with her."

"I don't think I do. What is she like?"

"She's exactly like her name. Don't you remember? Tall, very animated, glittering eyes, like the Ancient Mariner's?"

Niel laughed. "Don't you like bright eyes, Mrs. Forrester?"

"Not any others, I don't!" She joined in his laugh so gaily that the Captain looked out over his paper with an expression of satisfaction. He let the journal slowly crumple on his knees, and sat watching the two beside the grate. To him they seemed about the same age. It was a habit with him to think of Mrs. Forrester as very, very young.

She noticed that he was not reading. "Would you like me to light the lamp, Mr. Forrester?"

"No, thank you. The twilight is very pleasant."

It was twilight by now. They heard Mary come downstairs and begin stirring about the kitchen. The Captain, his slippers in the zone of firelight and his heavy shoulders in shadow, snored from time to time. As the room grew dusky, the windows were squares of clear, pale violet, and the shutters ceased to rattle. The wind was dying with the day. Everything was still, except when Bohemian Mary roughly clattered a pan. Mrs. Forrester whispered that she was out of sorts because her sweetheart, Joe Pucelik, hadn't been over to see her. Sunday night was his regular night, and Sunday was the first day of the blizzard. "When she's neglected, her tooth always begins to ache!"

"Well, now that I've got over, he'll have to come, or she will be in a temper."

"Oh, he'll come!" Mrs. Forrester shrugged. "I am blind and deaf, but I'm quite sure she makes it worth his while!" After a few moments she rose. "Come," she whispered, "Mr. Forrester is asleep. Let's run down the hill, there's no one to stop us. I'll slip on my rubber boots. No objections!" She put her fingers on his lips. "Not a word! I can't stand this house a moment longer."

They slipped quietly out of the front door into the cold air which tasted of new-fallen snow. A clear arc of blue and rose colour painted the west, over the buried town. When they reached the rounded breast of the hill, blown almost bare, Mrs. Forrester stood still and drew in deep breaths, looking down over the drifted meadows and the stiff, blue poplars.

"Oh, but it is bleak!" she murmured. "Suppose we should have to stay here all next winter, too, . . . and the next! What will become of me, Niel?" There was fear, unmistakable fright in her voice. "You see there is nothing for me to do. I get no exercise. I don't skate; we didn't in California, and my ankles are weak. I've always danced in the winter, there's plenty of dancing at Colorado Springs. You wouldn't believe how I miss it. I shall dance till I'm eighty. . . . I'll be the waltzing grandmother! It's good for me, I need it."

They plunged down into the drifts and did not stop again until they reached the wooden bridge

"See, even the creek is frozen! I thought running water never froze. How long will it be like this?"

"Not long now. In a month you'll see the

green begin in the marsh and run over the meadows. It's lovely over here in the spring. And you'll be able to get out tomorrow, Mrs. Forrester. The clouds are thinning. Look, there's the new moon!"

She turned. "Oh, I saw it over the wrong shoulder!"

"No you didn't. You saw it over mine."

She sighed and took his arm. "My dear boy, your shoulders aren't broad enough."

Instantly before his eyes rose the image of a pair of shoulders that were very broad, objectionably broad, clad in a frogged overcoat with an astrachan collar. The intrusion of this third person annoyed him as they went slowly back up the hill.

Curiously enough, it was as Captain Forrester's wife that she most interested Niel, and it was in her relation to her husband that he most admired her. Given her other charming attributes, her comprehension of a man like the railroad-builder, her loyalty to him, stamped her more than anything else. That, he felt, was quality; something that could never become worn or shabby; steel of Damascus. His admiration of Mrs. Forrester went back to that, just as, he felt, she herself went back to it. He rather liked the stories, even the spiteful ones, about the gay life she led in Colorado, and the young men she kept dangling about her every winter. He sometimes thought of the life she might have been living ever since he had known her,—and the one she had chosen to live. From that disparity, he believed, came the subtlest thrill of her fascination. She mocked outrageously at the proprieties she observed, and inherited the magic of contradictions.

VII

ON the evenings when there was no whist at the Forresters', Niel usually sat in his room and read,—but not law, as he was supposed to do. The winter before, when the Forresters were away, and one dull day dragged after another, he had come upon a copious diversion, an almost inexhaustible resource. The high, narrow bookcase in the back office, between the double doors and the wall, was filled from top to bottom with rows of solemn looking volumes bound in dark cloth, which were kept apart from the law library; an almost complete set of the Bohn classics, which Judge Pommeroy had bought long ago when he was a student at the University of Virginia. He had brought them West with him, not because he read them a great deal, but because, in his day, a gentleman had such books in his library, just as he had claret in his cellar. Among them was a set of Byron in three volumes, and last winter, apropos of a quotation which Niel didn't recognize, his uncle advised him to read Byron,—all except "Don Juan." That, the Judge remarked, with a deep smile, he "could save until later." Niel, of course, began with "Don Juan." Then he read "Tom Jones" and "Wilhelm Meister" and raced on until he came to Montaigne and a complete translation of Ovid. He hadn't finished yet with these last,—always went back to them after other experiments. These authors seemed to him to know their business. Even in "Don Juan" there was a little "fooling," but with these gentlemen none.

There were philosophical works in the collection, but he did no more than open and glance at them. He had no curiosity about what men had thought; but about what they had felt and lived, he had a great deal. If anyone had told him that these were classics and represented the wisdom of the ages, he would doubtless have let them alone. But ever since he had first found them for himself, he had been living a double life, with all its guilty enjoyments He read the *Heroides* over and over, and felt that they were the most glowing love stories ever told. He did not think of these books as something invented to beguile the idle hour, but as living creatures, caught in the very behaviour of living,—surprised behind their misleading severity of form and phrase. He was eavesdropping upon the past, being let into the great world that had plunged and glittered and sumptuously sinned long before little

Western towns were dreamed of. Those rapt evenings beside the lamp gave him a long perspective, influenced his conception of the people about him, made him know just what he wished his own relations with these people to be. For some reason, his reading made him wish to become an architect. If the Judge had left his Bohn library behind him in Kentucky, his nephew's life might have turned out differently.

Spring came at last, and the Forrester place had never been so lovely. The Captain spent long, happy days among his flowering shrubs, and his wife used to say to visitors, "Yes, you can see Mr. Forrester in a moment; I will send the English gardener to call him."

Early in June, when the Captain's roses were just coming on, his pleasant labors were interrupted. One morning an alarming telegram reached him. He cut it open with his garden shears, came into the house, and asked his wife to telephone for Judge Pommeroy. A savings bank, one in which he was largely interested, had failed in Denver. That evening the Captain and his lawyer went west on the express. The Judge, when he was giving Niel final instructions about the office business, told him he was afraid the Captain was bound to lose a good deal of money.

Mrs. Forrester seemed unaware of any danger; she went to the station to see her husband off, spoke of his errand merely as a "business trip." Niel, however, felt a foreboding gloom. He dreaded poverty for her. She was one of the people who ought always to have money; any retrenchment of their generous way of living would be a hardship for her,—would be unfitting. She would not be herself in straitened circumstances.

Niel took his meals at the town hotel; on the third day after Captain Forrester's departure, he was annoyed to find Frank Ellinger's name on the hotel register. Ellinger did not appear at supper, which meant, of course, that he was dining with Mrs. Forrester, and that the lady herself would get his dinner. She had taken the occasion of the Captain's absence to let Bohemian Mary go to visit her mother on the farm for a week. Niel thought it very bad taste in Ellinger to come to Sweet Water when Captain Forrester was away. He must know that it would stir up the gossips.

Niel had meant to call on Mrs. Forrester that evening, but now he went back to the office instead. He read late, and after he went to bed, he slept lightly. He was awakened before dawn by the puffing of the switch engine down at the round house. He tried to muffle his ears in the sheet and go to sleep again, but the sound of escaping steam for some reason excited him. He could not shut out the feeling that it was summer, and that the dawn would soon be flaming gloriously over the Forresters' marsh. He had awakened with that intense, blissful realization of summer which sometimes comes to children in their beds. He rose and dressed quickly. He would get over to the hill before Frank Ellinger could intrude his unwelcome presence, while he was still asleep in the best bedroom of the Wimbleton hotel.

An impulse of affection and guardianship drew Niel up the poplar-bordered road in the early light,—though he did not go near the house itself, but at the second bridge cut round through the meadow and on to the marsh. The sky was burning with the soft pink and silver of a cloudless summer dawn. The heavy, bowed grasses splashed him to the knees. All over the marsh, snow-on-the-mountain, globed with dew, made cool sheets of silver, and the swamp milk-weed spread its flat, raspberry-coloured clusters. There was an almost religious purity about the fresh morning air, the tender sky, the grass and flowers with the sheen of early dew upon them. There was in all living things something limpid and joyous—like the wet, morning call of the birds,

—84—

flying up through the unstained atmosphere. Out of the saffron east a thin, yellow, wine-like sunshine began to gild the fragrant meadows and the glistening tops of the grove. Niel wondered why he did not often come over like this, to see the day before men and their activities had spoiled it, while the morning was still unsullied, like a gift handed down from the heroic ages.

Under the bluffs that overhung the marsh he came upon thickets of wild roses, with flaming buds, just beginning to open. Where they had opened, their petals were stained with that burning rose-colour which is always gone by noon,—a dye made of sunlight and morning and moisture, so intense that it cannot possibly last . . . must fade, like ecstasy. Niel took out his knife and began to cut the stiff stems, crowded with red thorns.

He would make a bouquet for a lovely lady; a bouquet gathered off the cheeks of morning . . . these roses, only half awake, in the defencelessness of utter beauty. He would leave them just outside one of the French windows of her bedroom. When she opened her shutters to let in the light, she would find them,—and they would perhaps give her a sudden distaste for coarse worldlings like Frank Ellinger.

After tying his flowers with a twist of meadow grass, he went up the hill through the grove and softly round the still house to the north side of Mrs. Forrester's own room, where the door-like green shutters were closed. As he bent to place the flowers on the sill, he heard from within a woman's soft laughter; impatient, indulgent, teasing, eager. Then another laugh, very different, a man's. And it was fat and lazy, —ended in something like a yawn.

Niel found himself at the foot of the hill on the wooden bridge, his face hot, his temples beating, his eyes blind with anger. In his hand he still carried the prickly bunch of wild roses. He threw them over the wire fence into a mud-hole the cattle had trampled under the bank of the creek. He did not know whether he had left the house by the driveway or had come down through the shrubbery. In that instant between stooping to the window-sill and rising, he had lost one of the most beautiful things in his life. Before the dew dried, the morning had been wrecked for him; and all subsequent mornings, he told himself bitterly. This day saw the end of that admiration and loyalty that had been like a bloom on his existence. He could never recapture it. It was gone, like the morning freshness of the flowers.

"Lilies that fester," he muttered, *"lilies that fester smell far worse than weeds."*

Grace, variety, the lovely voice, the sparkle of fun and fancy in those dark eyes; all this was nothing. It was not a moral scruple she had outraged, but an aesthetic ideal. Beautiful women, whose beauty meant more than it said . . . was their brilliancy always fed by something coarse and concealed? Was that their secret?

VIII

NIEL met his uncle and Captain Forrester when they alighted from the morning train, and drove over to the house with them. The business on which they had gone to Denver was not referred to until they were sitting with Mrs. Forrester in the front parlour. The windows were open, and the perfume of the mock-orange and of June roses was blowing in from the garden. Captain Forrester introduced the subject, after slowly unfolding his handkerchief and wiping his forehead, and his fleshy neck, around his low collar.

"Maidy," he said, not looking at her, "I've come home a poor man. It took about everything there was to square up. You'll have this place, unencumbered, and my pension; that will be about all. The live-stock will bring in something."

Niel saw that Mrs. Forrester grew very pale, but she smiled and brought her husband his cigar stand. "Oh, well! I expect we can manage, can't we?"

"We can just manage. Not much more. I'm afraid Judge Pommeroy considers I acted foolishly."

"Not at all, Mrs. Forrester," the Judge exclaimed. "He acted just as I hope I would have done in his place. But I am an unmarried man. There were certain securities, government bonds, which Captain Forrester could have turned over to you, but it would have been at the expense of the depositors."

"I've known men to do that," said the Captain heavily, "but I never considered they paid their wives a compliment. If Mrs. Forrester is satisfied, I shall never regret my decision." For the first time his tired, swollen eyes sought his wife's.

"I never question your decisions in business, Mr. Forrester. I know nothing about such things."

The Captain put down the cigar he had taken but not lighted, rose with an effort, and walked over to the bay window, where he stood gazing out over his meadows. "The place looks very nice, Maidy," he said presently. "I see you've watered the roses. They need it, this weather. Now, if you'll excuse me, I'll lie down for a while. I did not sleep well on the train. Niel and the Judge will stay for lunch." He opened the door into Mrs. Forrester's room and closed it behind him.

Judge Pommeroy began to explain to Mrs. Forrester the situation they had faced in Denver. The bank, about which Mrs. Forrester knew nothing but its name, was one which paid good interest on small deposits. The depositors were wage-earners; railroad employés, mechanics, and day labourers, many of whom had at some time worked for Captain Forrester. His was the only well-known name among the bank officers, it was the name which promised security and fair treatment to his old workmen and their friends. The other directors were promising young business men with many irons in the fire. But, the Judge said with evident chagrin, they had refused to come up to the scratch and pay their losses like gentlemen. They claimed that the bank was insolvent, not through unwise investments or mismanagement, but because of a nation-wide financial panic, a shrinking in values that no one could have foreseen. They argued that the fair thing was to share the loss with the depositors; to pay them fifty cents on the dollar, giving long-time notes for twenty-five per cent, settling on a basis of seventy-five per cent.

Captain Forrester had stood firm that not one of the depositors should lose a dollar. The promising young business men had listened to him respectfully, but finally told him they would settle only on their own terms; any additional refunding must be his affair. He sent to the vault for his private steel box, opened it in their presence, and sorted the contents on the table. The government bonds he turned in at once. Judge Pommeroy was sent out to sell the mining stocks and other securities in the open market.

At this part of his narrative the Judge rose and began to pace the floor, twisting the seals on his watchchain. "That was what a man of honour was bound to do, Mrs. Forrester. With five of the directors backing down, he had either to lose his name or save it. The depositors had put their savings into that bank because Captain Forrester was president. To those men with no capital but their back and their two hands, his name meant safety. As he tried to explain to the directors, those deposits were above price; money saved to buy a home, or to take care of a man in sickness, or to send a boy to school. And those young men, bright fellows, well thought of in the community, sat there and looked down their noses and let your husband strip himself down to pledging his life insurance! There was a crowd in the street outside the bank all day, every day; Poles and Swedes and Mexicans, looking scared

to death.   A lot of them couldn't speak English,
—seemed like the only English word they knew
was 'Forrester.'   As we went in and out we'd
hear the Mexicans saying, 'Forrester, Forrester.'
It was a torment for me, on your account, Ma'm,
to see the Captain strip himself.   But, 'pon my
honour, I couldn't forbid him.   As for those
white-livered rascals that sat there,—" the Judge
stopped before Mrs. Forrester and ruffled his
bushy white hair with both hands, "By God,
Madam, I think I've lived too long!   In my day
the difference between a business man and a
scoundrel was bigger than the difference between
a white man and a nigger.   I wasn't the right one
to go out there as the Captain's counsel.   One of
these smooth members of the bar, like Ivy Peters
is getting ready to be, might have saved something for you out of the wreck.   But I couldn't
use my influence with your husband.   To that
crowd outside the bank doors his name meant a
hundred cents on the dollar, and by God, they
got it!   I'm proud of him, Ma'm; proud of his
acquaintance!"

It was the first time Niel had ever seen Mrs.
Forrester flush.   A quick pink swept over her
face.   Her eyes glistened with moisture.   "You
were quite right, Judge.   I wouldn't for the world
have had him do otherwise for me.   He would

never hold up his head again. You see, I know him." As she said this she looked at Niel, on the other side of the room, and her glance was like a delicate and very dignified rebuke to some discourtesy,—though he was not conscious of having shown her any.

When their hostess went out to see about lunch, Judge Pommeroy turned to his nephew. "Son, I'm glad you want to be an archi†ect. I can't see any honourable career for a lawyer, in this new business world that's coming up. Leave the law to boys like Ivy Peters, and get into some clean profession. I wasn't the right man to go with Forrester." He shook his head sadly.

"Will they really be poor?"

"They'll be pinched. It's as he said; they've nothing left but this place."

Mrs. Forrester returned and went to waken her husband for lunch. When she opened the door into her room, they heard stertorous breathing, and she called to them to come quickly. The Captain was stretched upon his iron bed in the antechamber, and Mrs. Forrester was struggling to lift his head.

"Quick, Niel," she panted. "We must get pillows under him. Bring those from my bed."

Niel gently pushed her away. Sweat poured from his face as he got his strength under the Captain's shoulders. It was like lifting a wounded elephant. Judge Pommeroy hurried back to the sitting-room and telephoned Dr. Dennison that Captain Forrester had had a stroke.

A stroke could not finish a man like Daniel Forrester. He was kept in his bed for three weeks, and Niel helped Mrs. Forrester and Ben Keezer take care of him. Although he was at the house so much during that time, he never saw Mrs. Forrester alone,—scarcely saw her at all, indeed. With so much to attend to, she became abstracted, almost impersonal. There were many letters to answer, gifts of fruit and wine and flowers to be acknowledged. Solicitous inquiries came from friends scattered all the way from the Missouri to the mountains. When Mrs. Forrester was not in the Captain's room, or in the kitchen preparing special foods for him, she was at her desk.

One morning while she was seated there, a distinguished visitor arrived. Niel, waiting by the door for the letters he was to take to the post, saw a large, red-whiskered man in a rumpled pongee suit and a panama hat come climbing up the hill; Cyrus Dalzell, president of the Colorado & Utah, who had come over in his private car to enquire for the health of his old friend

Niel warned Mrs. Forrester, and she went to meet the visitor, just as he mounted the steps, wiping his face with a red silk bandanna.

He took both the lady's hands and exclaimed in a warm, deep voice, "Here she is, looking as fresh as a bride! May I claim an old privilege?" He bent his head and kissed her. "I won't be in your way, Marian," he said as they came into the house, "but I had to see for myself how he does, and how you do."

Mr. Dalzell shook hands with Niel, and as he talked he moved about the parlour clumsily and softly, like a brown bear. Mrs. Forrester stopped him to straighten his flowing yellow tie and pull down the back of his wrinkled coat. "It's easy to see that Kitty wasn't with you this morning when you dressed," she laughed.

"Thank you, thank you, my dear. I've got a green porter down there, and he doesn't seem to realize the extent of his duties. No, Kitty wanted to come, but we have two giddy nieces out from Portsmouth, visiting us, and she felt she couldn't. I just had my car hitched on to the tail of the Burlington flyer and came myself. Now tell me about Daniel. Was it a stroke?"

Mrs. Forrester sat down on the sofa beside him and told him about her husband's illness, while he interrupted with sympathetic questions and comments, taking her hand between his large, soft palms and patting it affectionately.

"And now I can go home and tell Kitty that 'ie will soon be as good as ever,—and that you look like you were going to lead the ball tonight. You whisper to Daniel that I've got a couple cases of port down in my car that will build him up faster th... anything the doctors give him. And I've brought along a dozen sherry, for a lady that knows a thing or two about wines. And next winter you are both coming out to stay with us at the Springs, for a change of air."

Mrs. Forrester shook her head gently. "Oh, that, I'm afraid, is a pretty dream. But we'll dream it, anyway!" Everything about her had brightened since Cyrus Dalzell came up the hill. Even the long garnet earrings beside her cheeks seemed to flash with a deeper colour, Niel thought. She was a different woman from the one who sat there writing, half an hour ago. Her fingers, as they played on the sleeve of the pongee coat, were light and fluttery as butterfly wings.

"No dream at all, my dear. Kitty has arranged everything. You know how quickly she thinks things out. I am to come for you in my car. We'll get my old porter Jim as a valet for Daniel, and you can just play around and put fresh life into us all. We saw last winter that we couldn't do anything without our Lady Forrester. Nothing came off right without her. If we had a party, we sat down afterward and wondered what in hell we'd had it for. Oh, no, we can't manage without you!"

Tears flashed into her eyes. "That's very dear of you. It's sweet to be remembered when one is away." In her voice there was the heart-breaking sweetness one sometimes hears in lovely, gentle old songs.

IX

AFTER three weeks the Captain was up and around again. He dragged his left foot, and his left arm was uncertain. Though he recovered his speech, it was thick and clouded; some words he could not pronounce distinctly,— slid over them, dropped out a syllable. Therefore he avoided talking even more than was his habit. The doctor said that unless another brain lesion occurred, he might get on comfortably for some years yet.

In August Niel was to go to Boston to begin coaching for his entrance examinations at the Massachusetts Institute of Technology, where he meant to study architecture. He put off bidding the Forresters good-bye until the very day before he left. His last call was different from any he had ever made there before. Already they began to treat him like a young man. He sat rather stiffly in that parlour where he had been so much at home. The Captain was in his big chair in the bay window, in the full glow of the afternoon sun, saying little, but very friendly. Mrs. Forrester, on the sofa in the shadowy corner of the room, talked about Niel's plans and his journey.

"Is it true that Mary is going to marry Puce-lik this fall?" he asked her. "Who will you get to help you?"

"No one, for the present. Ben will do all I can't do. Never mind us. We will pass a quiet winter, like an old country couple,—as we are!" she said lightly.

Niel knew that she faced the winter with terror, but he had never seen her more in command of herself,—or more the mistress of her own house than now, when she was preparing to become the servant of it. He had the feeling, which he never used to have, that her lightness cost her something.

"Don't forget us, but don't mope. Make lots of new friends. You'll never be twenty again. Take a chorus girl out to supper—a pretty one, mind! Don't bother about your allowance. If you got into a scrape, we could manage a little cheque to help you out, couldn't we, Mr. Forrester?"

The Captain puffed and looked amused. "I think we could, Niel, I think so. Don't get up, my boy. You must stay to dinner."

Niel said he couldn't. He hadn't finished packing, and he was leaving on the morning train.

"Then we must have a little something before you go." Captain Forrester rose heavily, with the aid of his cane, and went into the dining-room. He brought back the decanter and filled three glasses with ceremony. Lifting his glass, he paused, as always, and blinked.

"Happy days!"

"Happy days!" echoed Mrs. Forrester, with her loveliest smile, "and every success to Niel!"

Both the Captain and his wife came to the door with him, and stood there on the porch together, where he had so often seen them stand to speed the parting guest. He went down the hill touched and happy. As he passed over the bridge his spirits suddenly fell. Would that chilling doubt always lie in wait for him, down there in the mud, where he had thrown his roses one morning?

He burned to ask her one question, to get the truth out of her and set his mind at rest: What did she do with all her exquisiteness when she was with a man like Ellinger? Where did she put it away? And having put it away, how could she recover herself, and give one—give even him— the sense of tempered steel, a blade that could fence with anyone and never break?

PART TWO

I

IT was two years before Niel Herbert came home again, and when he came the first acquaintance he met was Ivy Peters. Ivy got on the train at one of the little stations east of Sweet Water, where he had been trying a case. As he strolled through the Pullman he noticed among the passengers a young man in a grey flannel suit, with a silk shirt of one shade of blue and a necktie of another. After regarding this urban figure from the rear for a few seconds, Ivy glanced down at his own clothes with gloating satisfaction. It was a hot day in June, but he wore the black felt hat and ready-made coat of winter weight he had always affected as a boy. He stepped forward, his hands thrust in his pockets.

"Hullo, Niel. Thought I couldn't be mistaken."

Niel looked up and saw the red, bee-stung face, with its two permanent dimples, smiling down at him in contemptuous jocularity.

"Hello, Ivy. I couldn't be mistaken in you, either."

"Coming home to go into business?"

Niel replied that he was coming only for the summer vacation.

"Oh, you're not through school yet? I suppose it takes longer to make an architect than it does to make a shyster. Just as well; there's not much building going on in Sweet Water these days. You'll find a good many changes."

"Won't you sit down?" Niel indicated the neighbouring chair. "You are practising law?"

"Yes, along with a few other things. Have to keep more than one iron in the fire to make a living with us. I farm a little on the side. I rent that meadow-land on the Forrester place. I've drained the old marsh and put it into wheat. My brother John does the work, and I boss the job. It's quite profitable. I pay them a good rent, and they need it. I doubt if they could get along without. Their influential friends don't seem to help them out much. Remember all those chesty old boys the Captain used to drive about in his democrat wagon, and ship in barrels of Bourbon for? Good deal of bluff about all those old-timers. The panic put them out of the game. The Forresters have come down in the world like the rest. You remember how the old man used to put it over us kids and not let us carry a gun in there? I'm just mean enough to like to shoot along that creek a little better than anywhere else, now. There wasn't any harm in the old Captain, but he had the delusion of grandeur. He's happier now that he's like the rest of us and don't have to change his shirt every day." Ivy's unblinking greenish eyes rested upon Niel's haberdashery.

Niel, however, did not notice this. He knew that Ivy wanted him to show disappointment, and he was determined not to do so. He enquired about the Captain's health, pointedly keeping Mrs. Forrester's name out of the conversation.

"He's only about half there . . . seems contented enough. . . . She takes good care of him, I'll say that for her. . . . She seeks consolation, always did, you know . . . too much French brandy . . . but she never neglects him. I don't blame her. Real work comes hard on her."

Niel heard these remarks dully, through the buzz of an idea. He felt that Ivy had drained the marsh quite as much to spite him and Mrs. Forrester as to reclaim the land. Moreover, he seemed to know that until this moment Ivy him-

self had not realized how much that consideration weighed with him. He and Ivy had disliked
each other from childhood, blindly, instinctively,
recognizing each other through antipathy, as
hostile insects do. By draining the marsh Ivy
had obliterated a few acres of something he hated,
though he could not name it, and had asserted his
power over the people who had loved those un-
productive meadows for their idleness and silvery
beauty.

After Ivy had gone on into the smoker, Niel
sat looking out at the windings of the Sweet Water
and playing with his idea. The Old West had
been settled by dreamers, great-hearted adven-
turers who were unpractical to the point of mag-
nificence; a courteous brotherhood, strong in at-
tack but weak in defence, who could conquer but
could not hold. Now all the vast territory they
had won was to be at the mercy of men like Ivy
Peters, who had never dared anything, never
risked anything. They would drink up the mir-
age, dispel the morning freshness, root out the
great brooding spirit of freedom, the generous,
easy life of the great land-holders. The space,
the colour, the princely carelessness of the pioneer
they would destroy and cut up into profitable bits,
as the match factory splinters the primeval forest.
All the way from the Missouri to the mountains

this generation of shrewd young men, trained to petty economies by hard times, would do exactly what Ivy Peters had done when he drained the Forrester marsh.

II

THE next afternoon Niel found Captain Forrester in the bushy little plot he called his rose garden, seated in a stout hickory chair that could be left out in all weather, his two canes beside him. His attention was fixed upon a red block of Colorado sandstone, set on a granite boulder in the middle of the gravel space around which the roses grew. He showed Niel that this was a sun-dial, and explained it with great pride. Last summer, he said, he sat out here a great deal, with a square board mounted on a post, and marked the length of the shadows by his watch. His friend, Cyrus Dalzell, on one of his visits, took this board away, had the diagram exactly copied on sandstone, and sent it to him, with the column-like boulder that formed its base.

"I think it's likely Mr. Dalzell hunted around among the mountains a good many mornings before he found a natural formation like that," said the Captain. "A pillar, such as they had in Bible times. It's from the Garden of the Gods. Mr. Dalzell has his summer home up there."

The Captain sat with the soles of his boots together, his legs bowed out. Everything about him seemed to have grown heavier and weaker. His face was fatter and smoother; as if the features were running into each other, as when a wax face melts in the heat. An old Panama hat, burned yellow by the sun, shaded his eyes. His brown hands lay on his knees, the fingers well apart, nerveless. His moustache was the same straw colour; Niel remarked to him that it had grown no grayer. The Captain touched his cheek with his palm. "Mrs. Forrester shaved me for awhile. She did it very nicely, but I didn't like to have her do it. Now I use one of these safety razors. I can manage, if I take my time. The barber comes over once a week. Mrs. Forrester is expecting you, Niel. She's down in the grove. She goes down there to rest in the hammock."

Niel went round the house to the gate that gave into the grove. From the top of the hill he could see the hammock slung between two cottonwoods, in the low glade at the farther end, where he had fallen the time he broke his arm. The slender white figure was still, and as he hurried across the grass he saw that a white garden hat lay over her face. He approached quietly and was just wondering if she were asleep, when he heard a soft, delighted laugh, and with a quick movement she threw off the lace hat through which she had been watching him. He stepped forward and caught her suspended figure, hammock and all, in his arms. How light and alive she was! like a bird caught in a net. If only he could rescue her and carry her off like this,—off the earth of sad, inevitable periods, away from age, weariness, adverse fortune!

She showed no impatience to be released, but lay laughing up at him with that gleam of something elegantly wild, something fantastic and tantalizing,—seemingly so artless, really the most finished artifice! She put her hand under his chin as if he were still a boy.

"And how handsome he's grown! Isn't the old Judge proud of you! He called me up last night and began sputtering, 'It's only fair to warn you, Ma'm, that I've a very handsome boy over here.' As if I hadn't known you would be! And now you're a man, and have seen the world! Well, what have you found in it?"

"Nothing so nice as you, Mrs. Forrester."

"Nonsense! You have sweethearts?"

"Perhaps."

"Are they pretty?"

"Why they? Isn't one enough?"

"One is too many. I want you to have half a dozen,—and still save the best for us! One would take everything. If you had her, you would not have come home at all. I wonder if you know how we've looked for you?" She took his hand and turned a seal ring about on his little finger absently. "Every night for weeks, when the lights of the train came swinging in down below the meadows, I've said to myself, 'Niel is coming home; there's that to look forward to.'" She caught herself as she always did when she found that she was telling too much, and finished in a playful tone. "So, you see, you mean a great deal to all of us. Did you find Mr. Forrester?"

"Oh, yes! I had to stop and look at his sundial."

She raised herself on her elbow and lowered her voice. "Niel, can you understand it? He isn't childish, as some people say, but he will sit and watch that thing hour after hour. How can anybody like to see time visibly devoured? We are all used to seeing clocks go round, but why does he want to see that shadow creep on that stone? Has he changed much? No? I'm glad you feel so. Now tell me about the Adamses and what George is like."

Niel dropped on the turf and sat with his back against a tree trunk, answering her rapid questions and watching her while he talked. Of course, she was older. In the brilliant sun of the afternoon one saw that her skin was no longer like white lilacs,—it had the ivory tint of gardenias that have just begun to fade. The coil of blue-black hair seemed more than ever too heavy for her head. There were lines,—something strained about the corners of her mouth that used not to be there. But the astonishing thing was how these changes could vanish in a moment, be utterly wiped out in a flash of personality, and one forgot everything about her except herself.

"And tell me, Niel, do women really smoke after dinner now with the men, nice women? I shouldn't like it. It's all very well for actresses, but women can't be attractive if they do everything that men do."

"I think just now it's the fashion for women to make themselves comfortable, before anything else."

Mrs. Forrester glanced at him as if he had said something shocking. "Ah, that's just it! The two things don't go together. Athletics and going to college and smoking after dinner—Do you like it? Don't men like women to be different from themselves? They used to."

Niel laughed. Yes, that was certainly the idea of Mrs. Forrester's generation.

"Uncle Judge says you don't come to see him

any more as you used to, Mrs. Forrester. He misses it."

"My dear boy, I haven't been over to the town for six weeks. I'm always too tired. We have no horse now, and when I do go I have to walk. That house! Nothing is ever done there unless I do it, and nothing ever moves unless I move it. That's why I come down here in the afternoon,— to get where I can't see the house. I can't keep it up as it should be kept, I'm not strong enough. Oh, yes, Ben helps me; he sweeps and beats the rugs and washes windows, but that doesn't get a house very far." Mrs. Forrester sat up suddenly and pinned on her white hat. "We went all the way to Chicago, Niel, to buy that walnut furniture, couldn't find anything at home big and heavy enough. If I'd known that one day I'd have to push it about, I would have been more easily satisfied!" She rose and shook out her rumpled skirts.

They started toward the house, going slowly up the long, grassy undulation between the trees.

"Don't you miss the marsh?" Niel asked suddenly.

She glanced away evasively. "Not much. I would never have time to go there, and we need the money it pays us. And you haven't time to play any more either, Niel. You must hurry and become a successful man. Your uncle is terribly involved. He has been so careless that he's not much better off than we are. Money is a very important thing. Realize that in the beginning; face it, and don't be ridiculous in the end, like so many of us." They stopped by the gate at the top of the hill and looked back at the green alleys and the sharp shadows, at the quivering fans of light that seemed to push the trees farther apart and made Elysian fields underneath them. Mrs. Forrester put her white hand, with all its rings, on Niel's arm.

"Do you really find a kind of pleasure in coming back to us? That's very unusual, I think. At your age I wanted to be with the young and gay. It's nice for us, though." She looked at him with her rarest smile, one he had seldom seen on her face, but always remembered,—a smile without archness, without gaiety, full of affection and wistfully sad. And the same thing was in her voice when she spoke those quiet words,—the sudden quietness of deep feeling. She turned quickly away. They went through the gate and around the house to where the Captain sat watching the sunset glory on his roses. His wife touched his shoulder.

"Will you go in, now, Mr. Forrester, or shall I bring your coat?"

"I'll go in. Isn't Niel going to stay for dinner?"

"Not this time. He'll come soon, and we'll have a real dinner for him. Will you wait for Mr. Forrester, Niel? I must hurry in and start the fire."

Niel tarried behind and accompanied the Captain's slow progress toward the front of the house. He leaned upon two canes, lifting his feet slowly and putting them down firmly and carefully. He looked like an old tree walking.

Once up the steps and into the parlour, he sank into his big chair and panted heavily. The first whiff of a fresh cigar seemed to restore him. "Can I trouble you to mail some letters for me, Niel, as you go by the post-office?" He produced them from the breast pocket of his summer coat. "Let me see whether Mrs. Forrester has anything to go." Rising, the Captain went into the little hall. There, by the front door, on a table under the hatrack, was a scantily draped figure, an Arab or Egyptian slave girl, holding in her hands a large flat shell from the California coast. Niel remembered noticing that figure the first time he was ever in the house, when Dr. Dennison carried him out through this hallway with his arm in splints. In the days when the Forresters had servants and were sending over to

the town several times a day, the letters for the
post were always left in this shell. The Captain
found one now, and handed it to Niel. It was
addressed to Mr. Francis Bosworth Ellinger,
Glenwood Springs, Colorado.

For some reason Niel felt embarrassed and
tried to slip the letter quickly into his pocket.
The Captain, his two canes in one hand, prevented
him. He took the pale blue envelope again, and
held it out at arm's length, regarding it.

"Mrs. Forrester is a fine penman; have you
ever noticed? Always was. If she made me
a list of articles to get at the store, I never
had to hide it. It was like copper plate. That's
exceptional in a woman, Niel."

Niel remembered her hand well enough, he
had never seen another in the least like it; long,
thin, angular letters, curiously delicate and curiously bold, looped and laced with strokes fine as
a hair and perfectly distinct. Her script looked
as if it had been done at a high pitch of speed,
the pen driven by a perfectly confident dexterity.

"Oh, yes, Captain! I'm never able to take
any letters for Mrs. Forrester without looking at
them. No one could forget her writing."

"Yes. It's very exceptional." The Captain
gave him the envelope, and with his canes went
slowly toward his big chair.

Niel had often wondered just how much the Captain knew. Now, as he went down the hill, he felt sure that he knew everything; more than anyone else; all there was to know about Marian Forrester.

III

NIEL had planned to do a great deal of reading in the Forresters' grove that summer, but he did not go over so often as he had intended. The frequent appearance of Ivy Peters about the place irritated him. Ivy visited his new wheat fields on the bottom land very often; and he always took the old path, that led from what was once the marsh, up the steep bank and through the grove. He was likely to appear at any hour, his trousers stuffed into his top-boots, tramping along between the rows of trees with an air of proprietorship. He shut the gate behind the house with a slam and went whistling through the yard. Often he stopped at the kitchen door to call out some pleasantry to Mrs. Forrester. This annoyed Niel, for at that hour of the morning, when she was doing her house-work, Mrs. Forrester was not dressed to receive her inferiors. It was one thing to greet the president of the Colorado & Utah *en déshabille*, but it was another to chatter with a coarse-grained fellow like Ivy Peters in her wrapper and slippers, her sleeves rolled up and her throat bare to his cool, impudent eyes.

Sometimes Ivy strode through the rose plot where Captain Forrester was sitting in the sun,—went by without looking at him, as if there were no one there. If he spoke to the Captain at all, he did so as if he were addressing someone incapable of understanding anything. "Hullo, Captain, ain't afraid this sun will spoil your complexion?" or "Well, Captain, you'll have to get the prayer-meetings to take up this rain question. The drought's damned bad for my wheat."

One morning, as Niel was coming up through the grove, he heard laughter by the gate, and there he saw Ivy, with his gun, talking to Mrs. Forrester. She was bareheaded, her skirts blowing in the wind, her arm through the handle of a big tin bucket that rested on the fence beside her. Ivy stood with his hat on his head, but there was in his attitude that unmistakable something which shows that a man is trying to make himself agreeable to a woman. He was telling her a funny story, probably an improper one, for it brought out her naughtiest laugh, with something nervous and excited in it, as if he were going too far. At the end of his story Ivy himself broke into his farm-hand guffaw. Mrs. Forrester shook her finger at him and, catching up her pail, ran back into the house. She bent a little with its weight, but Ivy made no offer to carry it for her. He let her trip away with it as if she were a kitchen maid, and that were her business.

Niel emerged from the grove, and stopped where the Captain sat in the garden. "Good-morning, Captain Forrester. Was that Ivy Peters who just went through here? That fellow hasn't the manners of a pig!" he blurted out.

The Captain pointed to Mrs. Forrester's empty chair. "Sit down, Niel, sit down." He drew his handkerchief from his pocket and began polishing his glasses. "No, " he said quietly, "he ain't overly polite."

More than if he had complained bitterly, that guarded admission made one feel how much he had been hurt and offended by Ivy's rudeness. There was something very sad in his voice, and helpless. From his equals, respect had always come to him as his due; from fellows like Ivy he had been able to command it,—to order them off his place, or dismiss them from his employ.

Niel sat down and smoked a cigar with him. They had a long talk about the building of the Black Hills branch of the Burlington. In Boston last winter Niel had met an old mine-owner, who was living in Deadwood when the railroad first came in. When Niel asked him if he had known Daniel Forrester, the old gentleman said, "Forrester? Was he the one with the beautiful wife?"

"You must tell her," said the Captain, stroking the warm surface of his sun-dial. "Yes, indeed. You must tell Mrs. Forrester."

One night in the first week of July, a night of glorious moonlight, Niel found himself unable to read, or to stay indoors at all. He walked aimlessly down the wide, empty street, and crossed the first creek by the foot-bridge. The wide ripe fields, the whole country, seemed like a sleeping garden. One trod the dusty roads softly, not to disturb the deep slumber of the world.

In the Forrester lane the scent of sweet clover hung heavy. It had always grown tall and green here ever since Niel could remember; the Captain would never let it be cut until the weeds were mowed in the fall. The black, plume-like shadows of the poplars fell across the lane and over Ivy Peters' wheat fields. .As he walked on, Niel saw a white figure standing on the bridge over the second creek, motionless in the clear moonlight. He hurried forward. Mrs. Forrester was looking down at the water where it flowed bright over the pebbles. He came up beside her. "The Captain is asleep?"

"Oh, yes, long ago! He sleeps well, thank heaven! After I tuck him in, I have nothing more to worry about."

While they were standing there, talking in low voices, they heard a heavy door slam on the hill. Mrs. Forrester started and looked back over her shoulder. A man emerged from the shadow of the house and came striding down the drive-way. Ivy Peters stepped upon the bridge.

"Good evening," he said to Mrs. Forrester, neither calling her by name nor removing his hat. "I see you have company. I've just been up looking at the old barn, to see if the stalls are fit to put horses in there tomorrow. I'm going to start cutting wheat in the morning, and we'll have to put the horses in your stable at noon. We'd lose time taking them back to town."

"Why, certainly. The horses can go in our barn. I'm sure Mr. Forrester would have no objection." She spoke as if he had asked her permission.

"Oh!" Ivy shrugged. "The men will begin down here at six o'clock. I won't get over till about ten, and I have to meet a client at my office at three. Maybe you could give me some lunch, to save time."

His impudence made her smile. "Very well, then; I invite you to lunch. We lunch at one."

"Thanks. It will help me out." As if he had forgotten himself, he lifted his hat, and went down the lane swinging it in his hand.

Niel stood looking after him. "Why do you allow him to speak to you like that, Mrs. Forrester? If you'll let me, I'll give him a beating and teach him how to speak to you."

"No, no, Niel! Remember, we have to get along with Ivy Peters, we simply have to!" There was a note of anxiety in her voice, and she caught his arm.

"You don't have to take anything from him, or to stand his bad manners. Anybody else would pay you as much for the land as he does."

"But he has a lease for five years, and he could make it very disagreeable for us, don't you see? Besides," she spoke hurriedly, "there's more than that. He's invested a little money for me in Wyoming, in land. He gets splendid land from the Indians some way, for next to nothing. Don't tell your uncle; I've no doubt it's crooked. But the Judge is like Mr. Forrester; his methods don't work nowadays. He will never get us out of debt, dear man! He can't get himself out. Ivy Peters is terribly smart, you know. He owns half the town already."

"Not quite," said Niel grimly. "He's got hold of a good deal of property. He'll take advantage of anybody's necessity. You know he's utterly unscrupulous, don't you? Why didn't you let Mr. Dalzell, or some of your other old friends, invest your money for you?"

"Oh, it was too little! Only a few hundred dollars I'd saved on the housekeeping. They would put it into something safe, at six per cent. I know you don't like Ivy,—and he knows it! He's always at his worst before you. He's not so bad as—as his face, for instance!" She laughed nervously. "He honestly wants to help us out of the hole we're in. Coming and going all the time, as he does, he sees everything, and I really think he hates to have me work so hard."

"Next time you have anything to invest, you let me take it to Mr. Dalzell and explain. I'll promise to do as well by you as Ivy Peters can."

Mrs. Forrester took his arm and drew him into the lane. "But, my dear boy, you know nothing about these business schemes. You're not clever that way,—it's one of the things I love you for. I don't admire people who cheat Indians. Indeed I don't!" She shook her head vehemently.

"Mrs. Forrester, rascality isn't the only thing that succeeds in business."

"It succeeds faster than anything else, though," she murmured absently. They walked as far as the end of the lane and turned back again. Mrs.

Forrester's hand tightened on his arm. She began speaking abruptly. "You see, two years,
three years, more of this, and I could still go back
to California—and live again. But after
that . . . Perhaps people think I've settled down
to grow old gracefully, but I've not. I feel such a
power to live in me, Niel." Her slender fingers
gripped his wrist. "It's grown by being held
back. Last winter I was with the Dalzells at
Glenwood Springs for three weeks (I owe *that*
to Ivy Peters; he looked after things here, and his
sister kept house for Mr. Forrester), and I was
surprised at myself. I could dance all night and
not feel tired. I could ride horseback all day
and be ready for a dinner party in the evening.
I had no clothes, of course; old evening dresses
with yards and yards of satin and velvet in them,
that Mrs. Dalzell's sewing woman made over.
But I looked well enough! Yes, I did. I always
know how I'm looking, and I looked well enough.
The men thought so. I looked happier than any
woman there. They were nearly all younger,
much. But they seemed dull, bored to death.
After a glass or two of champagne they went to
sleep and had nothing to say! I always look
better after the first glass,—it gives me a little
colour, it's the only thing that does. I accepted
the Dalzell's invitation with a purpose; I wanted

to see whether I had anything left worth saving. And I have, I tell you! You would hardly believe it, I could hardly believe it, but I still have!"

By this time they had reached the bridge, a bare white floor in the moonlight. Mrs. Forrester had been quickening her pace all the while. "So that's what I'm struggling for, to get out of this hole,"—she looked about as if she had fallen into a deep well,—"out of it! When I'm alone here for months together, I plan and plot. If it weren't for that—"

As Niel walked back to his room behind the law offices, he felt frightened for her. When women began to talk about still feeling young, didn't it mean that something had broken? Two or three years, she said. He shivered. Only yesterday old Dr. Dennison had proudly told him that Captain Forrester might live a dozen. "We are keeping his general health up remarkably, and he was originally a man of iron."

What hope was there for her? He could still feel her hand upon his arm, as she urged him faster and faster up the lane.

IV

THE weather was dry and intensely hot for several weeks, and then, at the end of July, thunder-storms and torrential rains broke upon the Sweet Water valley. The river burst out of its banks, all the creeks were up, and the stubble of Ivy Peters' wheat fields lay under water. A wide lake and two rushing creeks now separated the Forresters from the town. Ben Keezer rode over to them every day to do the chores and to take them their mail. One evening Ben, with his slicker and leather mailbag, had just come out of the post-office and was preparing to mount his horse, when Niel Herbert stopped him to ask in a low voice whether he had got the Denver paper.

"Oh, yes. I always wait for the papers. She likes to have them to read of an evening. Guess it's pretty lonesome over there." He swung into his saddle and splashed off. Niel walked slowly around to the hotel for dinner. He had found something very disconcerting in the Denver paper: Frank Ellinger's picture on the society page, along with Constance Ogden's.

They had been married yesterday at Colorado Springs, and were stopping at the Antlers.

After supper Niel put on his rubber coat and started for the Forresters'. When he reached the first creek, he found that the foot-bridge had been washed out from the far bank and lay obliquely in the stream, battered at by the yellow current which might at any moment carry it away. One could not cross the ford without a horse. He looked irresolutely across the submerged bottom lands. The house was dark, no lights in the parlour windows. The rain was beginning to fall again. Perhaps she had rather be alone tonight. He would go over tomorrow.

He went back to the law office and tried to make himself comfortable, though the place was in distracting disorder. The continued rain had set one of the chimneys leaking, had brought down streams of soot and black water and flooded the stove and the Judge's once handsome Brussels carpet. The tinner had been there all afternoon, trying to find what was the matter with the flue, cutting a new sheet-iron drawer to fit under the stove-pipe. But at six o'clock he had gone away, leaving tools and sheets of metal lying about. The rooms were damp and cold. Niel put on a heavy sweater, since he could not have a fire, lit the big coal-oil lamp, and sat down with a book. When at last he looked at his watch, it was nearly midnight, and he had been reading three hours. He would have another pipe, and go to bed. He had scarcely lit it, when he heard quick, hurrying footsteps in the echoing corridor outside. He got to the door in an instant, was there to open it before Mrs. Forrester had time to knock. He caught her by the arm and pulled her in.

Everything but her wet, white face was hidden by a black rubber hat and a coat that was much too big for her. Streams of water trickled from the coat, and when she opened it he saw that she was drenched to the waist,—her black dress clung in a muddy pulp about her.

"Mrs. Forrester," he cried, "you can't have crossed the creek! It's up to a horse's belly in the ford."

"I came over the bridge, what's left of it. It shook under me, but I'm not heavy." She threw off her hat and wiped the water from her face with her hands.

"Why didn't you ask Ben to bring you over on his horse? Here, please swallow this."

She pushed his hand aside. "Wait. Afterwards. Ben? I didn't think until after he was gone. It's the telephone I want, long distance.

—129—

Get me Colorado Springs, the Antlers, quick!"

Then Niel noticed that she smelled strong of spirits; it steamed above the smell of rubber and creek mud and wet cloth. She snatched up the desk telephone, but he gently took it from her.

"I'll get them for you, but you're in no condition to talk now; you're out of breath. Do you really want to talk tonight? You know Mrs. Beasley will hear every word you say." Mrs. Beasley was the Sweet Water central, and an indefatigable reporter of everything that went over the wires.

Mrs. Forrester, sitting in his uncle's desk chair, tapped the carpet with the toe of her rubber boot. "Do hurry, please," she said in that polite, warning tone of which even Ivy Peters was afraid.

Niel aroused the sleepy central and put in the call. "She asks whom you wish to speak to?"

"Frank Ellinger. Say Judge Pommeroy's office wishes to speak to him."

Niel began soothing Mrs. Beasley at the other end. "No, not the management, Mrs. Beasley, one of the guests. Frank Ellinger," he spelled the name. "Yes. Judge Pommeroy's office wants to talk to him. I'll be right here. As soon as you can, please."

He put down the instrument. "I'd rather, you

know, publish anything in the town paper than telephone it through Mrs. Beasley." Mrs. Forrester paid no heed to him, did not look at him, sat staring at the wall. "I can't see why you didn't call me up and ask me to bring a horse over for you, if you felt you must get to a long distance telephone tonight."

"Yes; I didn't think of it. I only knew I had to get over here, and I was afraid something might stop me." She was watching the telephone as if it were alive. Her eyes were shrunk to hard points. Her brows, drawn together in an acute angle, kept twitching in the frown which held them,—the singular frown of one overcome by alcohol or fatigue, who is holding on to consciousness by the strength of a single purpose. Her blue lips, the black shadows under her eyes, made her look as if some poison were at work in her body.

They waited and waited. Niel understood that she did not wish him to talk. Her mind was struggling with something, with every blink of her lashes she seemed to face it anew. Presently she rose as if she could bear the suspense no longer and went over to the window, leaned against it.

"Did you leave Captain Forrester alone?" Niel asked suddenly.

"Yes. Nothing will happen over there.

Nothing ever *does* happen!" she answered wildly, wringing her hands.

The telephone buzzed. Mrs. Forrester darted toward the desk, but Niel lifted the instrument in his left hand and barred her way with his right. "Try to be calm, Mrs. Forrester. When I get Ellinger I will let you talk to him,—and central will hear every word you say, remember."

After some exchanges with the Colorado office, he pointed her to the chair. "Sit down and I'll give it to you. He is on the wire."

He did not dare to leave her alone, though it was awkward enough to be a listener. He walked to the window and stood with his back to the desk where she was sitting.

"Is that you, Frank? This is Marian. I won't keep you a moment. You were asleep? So early? That's not like you. You've reformed already, haven't you? That's what marriage does, they say. No, I wasn't altogether surprised. You might have taken me into your confidence, though. Haven't I deserved it?"

A long, listening pause. Niel stared stupidly at the dark window. He had steeled his nerves for wild reproaches. The voice he heard behind him was her most charming; playful, affectionate, intimate, with a thrill of pleasant excite-

ment that warmed its slight formality and burned
through the common-place words like the colour in
an opal. He simply held his breath while she
fluttered on:

"Where shall you go for your honeymoon?
Oh, I'm very sorry! So soon . . . You must
take good care of her. Give her my love. . . .
I should think California, at this time of the year,
might be right . . ."

It went on like this for some minutes. The
voice, it seemed to Niel, was that of a woman,
young, beautiful, happy,—warm and at her ease,
sitting in her own drawing-room and talking on a
stormy night to a dear friend far away.

"Oh, unusually well, for me. Stop and see for
yourself. You will be going to Omaha on business next week, before California. Oh, yes, you
will! Stop off between trains. You know how
welcome you are, always."

A long pause. An exclamation from Mrs.
Forrester made Niel turn sharply round.
Now it was coming! Her voice was darkening
with every word. "I think I understand you.
You are not speaking from your own room?
What, from the office booth? Oh, then I understand you very well indeed!" Niel looked
about in alarm. It was time to stop her, but
how? The voice went on.

"Play safe! When have you ever played anything else? You know, Frank, the truth is that you're a coward; a great, hulking coward. Do you hear me? I want you to hear! . . . You've got a safe thing at last, I should think; safe and pasty! How much stock did you get with it? A big block, I hope! Now let me tell you the truth: I don't want you to come here! I never want to see you again while I live, and I forbid you to come and look at me when I'm dead. I don't want your hateful eyes to look at my dead face. Do you hear me? Why don't you answer me? Don't dare to hang up the receiver, you coward! Oh, you big . . . Frank, Frank, say something! Oh, he's shut me off, I can't hear him!"

She flung the receiver down, dropped her head on the desk, and broke into heavy, groaning sobs. Niel stood over her and waited with composure. For once he had been quick enough; he had saved her. The moment that quivering passion of hatred and wrong leaped into her voice, he had taken the big shears left by the tinner and cut the insulated wire behind the desk. Her reproaches had got no farther than this room.

When the sobs ceased he touched her shoulder. He shook her, but there was no response. She was asleep, sunk in a heavy stupor. Her hands and face were so cold that he thought there could not be a drop of warm blood left in her body. He carried her into his room, cut off her drenched clothing, wrapped her in his bathrobe and put her into his own bed. She was absolutely unconscious. He blew out the light, locked her in, and left the building, going as fast as he could to Judge Pommeroy's cottage. He roused his uncle and briefly explained the situation.

"Can you dress and go down to the office for the rest of the night, Uncle Judge? Some one must be with her. And I'll get over to the Captain at once; he certainly oughtn't to be left alone. If she could get across the bridge, I guess I can. By the way, she began talking wild, and I cut the telephone wire behind your desk. So keep an eye on it. It might make trouble on a stormy night like this. I'll get a livery hack and take Mrs. Forrester home in the morning, before the town is awake."

When daylight began to break Niel went into Captain Forrester's room and told him that his wife had been sent for in the night to answer a long distance telephone call, and that now he was going to bring her home.

The Captain lay propped up on three big pillows. Since his face had grown fat and relaxed, its ruggedness had changed to an almost Asiatic smoothness. He looked like a wise old

Chinese mandarin as he lay listening to the young man's fantastic story with perfect composure, merely blinking and saying, "Thank you, Niel, thank you."

As Niel went through the sleeping town on his way to the livery barn, he saw the short, plump figure of Mrs. Beasley, like a boiled pudding sewed up in a blue kimono, waddling through the feathery asparagus bed behind the telephone office. She had already been next door to tell her neighbour Molly Tucker, the seamstress, the story of her exciting night.

V

SOON afterward, when Captain Forrester had another stroke, Mrs. Beasley and Molly Tucker and their friends were perfectly agreed that it was a judgment upon his wife. No judgment could have been crueller. Under the care of him, now that he was helpless, Mrs. Forrester quite went to pieces.

Even after their misfortunes had begun to come upon them, she had maintained her old reserve. She had asked nothing and accepted nothing. Her demeanour toward the townspeople was always the same; easy, cordial, and impersonal. Her own friends had moved away long ago,— all except Judge Pommeroy and Dr. Dennison. When any of the housewives from the town came to call, she met them in the parlour, chatted with them in the smiling, careless manner they could never break through, and they got no further. They still felt they must put on their best dress and carry a card-case when they went to the Forresters'.

But now that the Captain was helpless, everything changed. She could hold off the curious no longer. The townswomen brought soups and custards for the invalid. When they came to sit out the night with him, she turned the house over to them. She was worn out; so exhausted that she was dull to what went on about her. The Mrs. Beasleys and Molly Tuckers had their chance at last. They went in and out of Mrs. Forrester's kitchen as familiarly as they did out of one another's. They rummaged through the linen closet to find more sheets, pried about in the attic and cellar. They went over the house like ants, the house where they had never before got past the parlour; and they found they had been fooled all these years. There was nothing remarkable about the place at all! The kitchen was inconvenient, the sink was smelly. The carpets were worn, the curtains faded, the clumsy, old-fashioned furniture they wouldn't have had for a gift, and the upstairs bed-rooms were full of dust and cobwebs.

Judge Pommeroy remarked to his nephew that he had never seen these women look so wide-awake, so important and pleased with themselves, as now when he encountered them bustling about the Forrester place. The Captain's illness had the effect of a social revival, like a new club or a church society. The creatures grew bolder and bolder,—and Mrs. Forrester, apparently, had no power of resistance. She drudged in the kitchen, slept, half-dressed, in one of the chambers upstairs, kept herself going on black coffee and brandy. All the bars were down. She had ceased to care about anything.

As the women came and went through the lane, Niel sometimes overheard snatches of their conversation.

"Why didn't she sell some of that silver? All those platters and covered dishes stuck away with the tarnish of years on them!"

"I wouldn't mind having some of her linen. There's a chest full of double damask upstairs, every tablecloth long enough to make two. Did you ever see anything like the wine glasses! I'll bet there's not as many in both saloons put together. If she has a sale after he's gone, I'll buy a dozen champagne glasses; they're nice to serve sherbet in."

"There are nine dozen glasses," said Molly Tucker, "counting them for beer and whiskey. If there is a sale, I've a mind to bid in a couple of them green ones, with long stems, for mantel ornaments. But she'll never sell 'em all, unless she can get the saloons to take 'em."

Ed Elliott's mother laughed. "She'll never sell 'em, as long as she's got anything to put in 'em."

"The cellar will go dry, some day."

"I guess there's always plenty that will get it for such as her. I never go there now that I don't smell it on her. I went over late the other night, and she was on her knees, washing up the kitchen floor. Her eyes were glassy. She kept washing the place around the ice-box over and over, till it made me nervous. I said, 'Mrs. Forrester, I think you've washed that place several times already.'"

"Was she confused?"

"Not a particle! She laughed and said she was often absent-minded."

Mrs. Elliott's companions laughed, too, and agreed that absent-minded was a good expression.

Niel repeated this conversation to his uncle. "Uncle," he declared, "I don't see how I can go back to Boston and leave the Forresters. I'd like to chuck school for a year, and see them through. I want to go over there and clear those gossips out. Could you stay at the hotel for a few weeks, and let me have Black Tom? With him to help me, I'd send every one of those women trotting down the lane."

It was arranged quietly, and at once. Tom was put in the kitchen, and Niel himself took charge of the nursing. He met the women with firmness: they were very kind, but now nothing was needed. The Doctor had said the house must be absolutely quiet and that the invalid must see no one.

Once the house was tranquil, Mrs. Forrester went to bed and slept for the better part of a week. The Captain himself improved. On his good days he could be put into a wheel-chair and rolled out into his garden to enjoy the September sunlight and the last of his briar roses.

"Thank you, Niel, thank you, Tom," he often said when they lifted him into his chair. "I value this quiet very highly." If a day came when they thought he ought not to go out, he was sad and disappointed.

"Better get him out, no matter what," said Mrs. Forrester. "He likes to look at his place. That, and his cigar, are the only pleasures he has left."

When she was rested and in command of herself again, she took her place in the kitchen, and Black Tom went back to the Judge.

At night, when he was alone, when Mrs. Forrester had gone to bed and the Captain was resting quietly, Niel found a kind of solemn happiness in his vigils. It had been hard to give up that year; most of his classmates were younger than he. It had cost him something, but now that he had taken the step, he was glad. As he put in the night hours, sitting first in one chair and then in another, reading, smoking, getting a lunch to keep himself awake, he had the satisfaction of those who keep faith. He liked being alone with the old things that had seemed so beautiful to him in his childhood. These were still the most comfortable chairs in the world, and he would never like any pictures so well as "William Tell's Chapel" and "The House of the Tragic Poet." No card-table was so good for solitaire as this old one with a stone top, mosaic in the pattern of a chess-board, which one of the Captain's friends had brought him from Naples. No other house could take the place of this one in his life.

He had time to think of many things; of himself and of his old friends here. He had noticed that often when Mrs. Forrester was about her work, the Captain would call to her, "Maidy, Maidy," and she would reply, "Yes, Mr. Forrester," from wherever she happened to be, but without coming to him,—as if she knew that when he called to her in that tone he was not asking for anything. He wanted to know if she were near, perhaps; or, perhaps, he merely liked to call her name and to hear her answer. The longer Niel was with Captain Forrester in those

peaceful closing days of his life, the more he
felt that the Captain knew his wife better even
than she knew herself; and that, knowing her,
he,—to use one of his own expressions,—valued
her.

VI

CAPTAIN FORRESTER'S death, which occurred early in December, was "telegraphic news," the only State news that the discouraged town of Sweet Water had furnished for a long while. Flowers and telegrams came from east and west, but it happened that none of the Captain's closest friends could come to his funeral. Mr. Dalzell was in California, the president of the Burlington railroad was travelling in Europe. The others were far away or in uncertain health. Doctor Dennison and Judge Pommeroy were the only two of his intimates among the pallbearers.

On the morning of the funeral, when the Captain was already in his coffin, and the undertaker was in the parlour setting up chairs, Niel heard a knocking at the kitchen door. There he found Adolph Blum, carrying a large white box.

"Niel," he said, "will you please give these to Mrs. Forrester, and tell her they are from Rhein and me, for the Captain?"

Adolph was in his old working clothes, the only clothes he had, probably, with a knitted comforter about his neck. Niel knew he wouldn't come to the funeral, so he said:

"Won't you come in and see him, 'Dolph? He looks just like himself."

Adolph hesitated, but he caught sight of the undertaker's man, through the parlour bay-window, and said, "No, thank you, Niel," thrust his red hands into his jacket pockets, and walked away.

Niel took the flowers out of the box, a great armful of yellow roses, which must have cost the price of many a dead rabbit. He carried them upstairs, where Mrs. Forrester was lying down.

"These are from the Blum boys," he said. "Adolph just brought them to the kitchen door."

Mrs. Forrester looked at them, then turned away her head on the pillow, her lips trembling. It was the only time that day he saw her pale composure break.

The funeral was large. Old settlers and farmer folk came from all over the county to follow the pioneer's body to the grave. As Niel and his uncle were driving back from the cemetery with Mrs. Forrester, she spoke for the first time since they had left the house. "Judge Pommeroy," she said quietly, "I think I will have Mr. Forrester's sun-dial taken over and put above his grave. I can have an inscription cut on the base. It seems more appropriate for him than any stone we could buy. And I will plant some of his own rose-bushes beside it."

When they got back to the house it was four o'clock, and she insisted upon making tea for them. "I would like it myself, and it is better to be doing something. Wait for me in the parlour. And, Niel, move the things back as we always have them."

The grey day was darkening, and as the three sat having their tea in the bay-window, swift squalls of snow were falling over the wide meadows between the hill and the town, and the creaking of the big cottonwoods about the house seemed to say that winter had come.

VII

ONE morning in April Niel was alone in the law office. His uncle had been ill with rheumatic fever for a long while, and he had been attending to the routine of business.

The door opened, and a figure stood there, strange and yet familiar,—he had to think a moment before he realized that it was Orville Ogden, who used to come to Sweet Water so often, but who had not been seen there now for several years. He didn't look a day older; one eye was still direct and clear, the other clouded and oblique. He still wore a stiff imperial and twisted moustache, the grey colour of old beeswax, and his thin hair was brushed heroically up over the bald spot.

"This is Judge Pommeroy's nephew, isn't it? I can't think of your name, my boy, but I remember you. Is the Judge out?"

"Please be seated, Mr. Ogden. My uncle is ill. He hasn't been at the office for several months. He's had really a very bad time of it. Is there anything I can do for you?"

"Oh, I'm sorry to hear that! I'm sorry." He spoke as if he were. "I guess all we fellows are getting older, whether we like it or not. It made a great difference when Daniel Forrester went." Mr. Ogden took off his overcoat, put his hat and gloves neatly on the desk, and then seemed somewhat at a loss. "What is your uncle's trouble?" he asked suddenly.

Niel told him. "I was to have gone back to school this winter, but uncle begged me to stay and look after things for him. There was no one here he wanted to entrust his business to."

"I see, I see," said Mr. Ogden thoughtfully. "Then you do attend to his business for the present?" He paused and reflected. "Yes, there was something that I wanted to take up with him. I am stopping off for a few hours only, between trains. I might speak to you about it, and you could consult your uncle and write me in Chicago. It's a confidential matter, and concerns another person."

Niel assured him of his discretion, but Mr. Ogden seemed to find the subject difficult to approach. He looked very grave and slowly lit a cigar.

"It is simply," he said at last, "a rather delicate suggestion I wish to make to your uncle about one of his clients. I have several friends in the Government at Washington just at present, friends who would go out of their way to serve me. I have been thinking that we might manage it to get a special increase of pension for Mrs. Forrester. I am due in Chicago this week, and after my business there is finished, I would be quite willing to go on to Washington to see what can be done; provided, of course, that no one, least of all your uncle's client, knows of my activity in the matter."

Niel flushed. "I'm sorry, Mr. Ogden," he brought out, "but Mrs. Forrester is no longer a client of my uncle's. After the Captain's death, she saw fit to take her business away from him."

Mr. Ogden's normal eye became as blank as the other.

"What's that? He isn't her lawyer? Why, for twenty years—"

"I know that, sir. She didn't treat him with much consideration. She transferred her business very abruptly."

"To whom, may I ask?"

"To a lawyer here in town; Ivy Peters."

"Peters? I never heard of him."

"No, you wouldn't have. He wasn't one of the people who went to the Forrester house in the old days. He's one of the younger generation, a few years older than I. He rented part of the Forresters' land for several years before the Captain's death,—was their tenant. That was how Mrs. Forrester came to know him. She thinks him a good business man."

Mr. Ogden frowned. "And is he?"

"Some people think so."

"Is he trustworthy?"

"Far from it. He takes the cases nobody else will take. He may treat Mrs. Forrester honestly. But if he does, it will not be from principle."

"This is very distressing news. Go on with your work, my boy. I must think this over." Mr. Ogden rose and walked about the room, his hands behind him. Niel turned to an unfinished letter on his desk, in order to leave his visitor the more free.

Mr. Ogden's position, he understood, was a difficult one. He had been devoted to Mrs. Forrester, and before Constance had made up her mind to marry Frank Ellinger, before the mother and daughter began to angle for him, Mr. Ogden had come to the Forresters' more frequently than any of their Denver friends. He hadn't been back, Niel believed, since that Christmas party when he and his family were there with Ellinger. Very soon afterward he must have seen what his women-folk were up to; and whether he approved or disapproved, he must have decided that there was nothing for him to do but to keep out. It hadn't been the Forresters' reversal of fortune that had kept him away. One could see that he was deeply troubled, that he had her heavily on his mind.

Niel had finished his letter and was beginning another, when Mr. Ogden stopped beside his desk, where he stood twisting his imperial tighter and tighter. "You say this young lawyer is unprincipled? Sometimes rascals have a soft spot, a sentiment, where women are concerned."

Niel stared. He immediately thought of Ivy's dimples.

"A soft spot? A sentiment? Mr. Ogden, why not go to his office? A glance would convince you."

"Oh, that's not necessary! I understand." He looked out of the window, from which he could just see the tree-tops of the Forrester grove, and murmured, "Poor lady! So misguided. She ought to have advice from some of Daniel's friends." He took out his watch and consulted it, turning something over in his mind. His train was due in an hour, he said. Nothing could be done at present. In a few moments he left the office.

Afterward, Niel felt sure that when Mr. Ogden stood there uncertainly, watch in hand, he was considering an interview with Mrs. Forrester. He had wanted to go to her, and had given it up. Was he afraid of his women-folk? Or was it another kind of cowardice, the fear of losing a pleasant memory, of finding her changed and marred, a dread of something that would throw a disenchanting light upon the past? Niel had heard his uncle say that Mr. Ogden admired pretty women, though he had married a homely one, and that in his deep, non-committal way he was very gallant. Perhaps, with a little encouragement, he would have gone to see Mrs. Forrester, and he might have helped her. The fact that he had done nothing to bring this about, made Niel realize how much his own feeling toward that lady had changed.

It was Mrs. Forrester herself who had changed. Since her husband's death she seemed to have become another woman. For years Niel and his uncle, the Dalzells and all her friends, had thought of the Captain as a drag upon his wife; a care that drained her and dimmed her and kept her from being all that she might be. But without him, she was like a ship without ballast, driven hither and thither by every wind. She was flighty and perverse. She seemed to have lost her faculty of discrimination; her power of easily and graciously keeping everyone in his proper place.

Ivy Peters had been in Wyoming at the time of Captain Forrester's illness and death,—called away by a telegram which announced that oil had been discovered near his land-holdings. He returned soon after the Captain's funeral, however, and was seen about the Forrester place more than ever. As there was nothing to be done on his fields in the winter, he had amused himself by pulling down the old barn after office hours. One was likely to come upon him, smoking his cigar on the front porch as if he owned the place. He often spent the evening there, playing cards with Mrs. Forrester or talking about his business projects. He had not made his fortune yet, but he was on the way to it. Occasionally he took a friend or two, some of the town boys, over to dine at Mrs. Forrester's. The boys' mothers and sweethearts were greatly scandalized. "Now she's after the young ones," said Ed Elliott's mother. "She's getting childish."

At last Niel had a plain talk with Mrs. Forrester. He told her that people were gossiping about Ivy's being there so much. He had heard comments even on the street.

"But I can't bother about their talk. They

have always talked about me, always will. Mr. Peters is my lawyer and my tenant; I have to see him, and I'm certainly not going to his office. I can't sit in the house alone every evening and knit. If you came to see me any oftener than you do, that would make talk. You are still younger than Ivy,—and better-looking! Did that never occur to you?"

"I wish you wouldn't talk to me like that," he said coldly. "Mrs. Forrester, why don't you go away? to California, to people of your own kind. You know this town is no place for you."

"I mean to, just as soon as I can sell this place. It's all I have, and if I leave it to tenants it will run down, and I can't sell it to advantage. That's why Ivy is here so much, he's trying to make the place presentable; pulling down the old barn that had become an eyesore, putting new boards in the porch floor where the old ones had rotted. Next summer, I am going to paint the house. Unless I keep the place up, I can never get my price for it." She talked nervously, with exaggerated earnestness, as if she were trying to persuade herself.

"And what are you asking for it now, Mrs. Forrester?"

"Twenty thousand dollars."

"You'll never get it. At least, not until times have greatly changed."

"That's what your uncle said. He wouldn't attempt to sell it for more than twelve. That's why I had to put it into other hands. Times have changed, but he doesn't realize it. Mr. Forrester himself told me it would be worth that. Ivy says he can get me twenty thousand, or if not, he will take it off my hands as soon as his investments begin to bring in returns."

"And in the meantime, you are simply wasting your life here."

"Not altogether. She looked at him with pleading plausibility. "I am getting rested after a long strain. And while I wait, I'm finding new friends among the young men,—those your age, and a little younger. I've wanted for a long while to do something for the boys in this town, but my hands were full. I hate to see them growing up like savages, when all they need is a civilized house to come to, and a woman to give them a few hints. They've never had a chance. You wouldn't be the boy you are if you'd never gone to Boston,—and you've always had older friends who'd seen better days. Suppose you had grown up like Ed Elliot and Joe Simpson?"

"I flatter myself I wouldn't be exactly like

them, if I had! However, there is no use discussing it, if you've thought it over and made up
your mind. I spoke of it because I thought
you mightn't realize how it strikes the townspeople."

"I know!" She tossed her head. Her eyes
glittered, but there was no mirth in them,—it was
more like hysterical defiance. "I know; they
call me the Merry Widow. I rather like it!"

Niel left the house without further argument,
and though that was three weeks ago, he had not
been back since. Mrs. Forrester had called to
see his uncle in the meantime. The Judge was
as courtly as ever in his manner toward her, but
he was deeply hurt by her defection, and his
cherishing care for her would never be revived.
He had attended to all Captain Forrester's business for twenty years, and since the failure of
the Denver bank had never deducted a penny for
fees from the money entrusted to him. Mrs.
Forrester had treated him very badly. She had
given him no warning. One day Ivy Peters had
come into the office with a written order from
her, requesting that an accounting, and all funds
and securities, be turned over to him. Since then
she had never spoken of the matter to the Judge,
—or to Niel, save in that conversation about
the sale of the property.

VIII

ONE morning when a warm May wind was whirling the dust up the street, Mrs. Forrester came smiling into Judge Pommeroy's office, wearing a new spring bonnet, and a short black velvet cape, fastened at the neck with a bunch of violets. "Please be nice enough to notice my new clothes, Niel," she said coaxingly. "They are the first I've had in years and years."

He told her they were very pretty.

"And aren't you glad I have some at last?" she smiled enquiringly through her veil. "I feel as if you weren't going to be cross with me today, and would do what I ask you. It's nothing very troublesome. I want you to come to dinner Friday night. If you come, there will be eight of us, counting Annie Peters. They are all boys you know, and if you don't like them, you ought to! Yes, you ought to!" she nodded at him severely. "Since you mind what people say, Niel, aren't you afraid they'll be saying you're a snob, just because you've been to Boston and seen a little of the world? You mustn't be so stiff, so—

—157—

so superior! It isn't becoming, at your age."
She drew her brows down into a level frown so
like his own that he laughed. He had almost
forgotten her old talent for mimicry.

"What do you want me for? You used always
to say it was no good asking people who didn't
mix."

"You can mix well enough, if you take the
trouble. And this time you will, for me. Won't
you?"

When she was gone, Niel was angry with himself for having been persuaded.

On Friday evening he was the last guest to ar-
rive. It was a warm night, after a hot day.
The windows were open, and the perfume of
the lilacs came into the dusky parlour where the
boys were sitting about in chairs that seemed too
big for them. A lamp was burning in the dining-
room, and there Ivy Peters stood at the sideboard, mixing cocktails. His sister Annie was in
the kitchen, helping the hostess. Mrs. Forrester
came in for a moment to greet Niel, then ex-
cused herself and hurried back to Annie Peters.
Through the open door he saw that the silver
dishes had reappeared on the dinner table, and
the candlesticks and flowers. The young men
who sat about in the twilight would not know the
difference, he thought, if she had furnished her

table that morning, from the stock in Wernz's queensware store. Their conception of a really fine dinner service was one "hand painted" by a sister or sweetheart. Each boy sat with his legs crossed, one tan shoe swinging in the air and displaying a tan silk sock. They were talking about clothes; Joe Simpson, who had just inherited his father's clothing business, was eager to tell them what the summer styles would be.

Ivy Peters came in, shaking his drinks. "You fellows are like a bunch of girls,—always talking about what you are going to wear and how you can spend your money. Simpson wouldn't get rich very fast if you all wore your clothes as long as I do. When did I get this suit, Joe?"

"Oh, about the year I graduated from High School, I guess!"

They all laughed at Ivy. No matter what he did or said, they laughed,—in recognition of his general success.

Mrs. Forrester came back, fanning herself with a little sandalwood fan, and when she appeared the boys rose,—in alarm, one might have thought, from the suddenness of it. That much, at any rate, she had succeeded in teaching them.

"Are your cocktails ready, Ivy? You will have to wait for me a moment, while I put some powder on my nose. If I'd known how hot it would be tonight, I'm afraid I wouldn't have had a roast for you. I'm browner than the ducks. You can pour them though. I won't be long."

She disappeared into her own room, and the boys sat down with the same surprising promptness. Ivy Peters carried the tray about, and they held their glasses before them, waiting for Mrs. Forrester. When she came, she took Niel's arm and led him into the dining-room. "Did you notice," she whispered to him, "how they hold their glasses? What is it they do to a little glass to make it look so vulgar? Nobody could ever teach them to pick one up and drink out of it, not if there were tea in it!"

Aloud she said, "Niel, will you light the candles for me? And then take the head of the table, please. You can carve ducks?"

"Not so well as—as my uncle does," he murmured, carefully putting back a candle-shade.

"Nor as Mr. Forrester did? I don't ask that. Nobody can carve now as men used to. But you can get them apart, I suppose? The place at your right is for Annie Peters. She is bringing in the dinner for me. Be seated, gentlemen!" with a little mocking bow and a swinging of earrings.

While Niel was carving the ducks, Annie slipped into the chair beside him, her naturally red face glowing from the heat of the stove. She was several years younger than her brother, whom she obeyed unquestioningly in everything. She had an extremely bad complexion and pale yellow hair with white lights in it, exactly the colour of molasses taffy that has been pulled unti. it glistens. During the dinner she did not once speak, except to say, "Thank you," or "No, thank you." Nobody but Mrs. Forrester talked much until the first helping of duck was consumed. The boys had not yet learned to do two things at once. They paused only to ask their hostess if she "would care for the jelly," or to answer her questions.

Niel studied Mrs. Forrester between the candles, as she nodded encouragingly to one and another, trying to "draw them out," laughing at Roy Jones' heavy jokes, or congratulating Joe Simpson upon his new dignity as a business man with a business of his own. The long earrings swung beside the thin cheeks that were none the better, he thought, for the rouge she had put on them when she went to her room just before dinner. It improved some women, but not her, —at least, not tonight, when her eyes were hollow with fatigue, and she looked pinched and worn as he had never seen her. He sighed as he thought how much work it meant to cook a din-

ner like this for eight people,—and a beefsteak
with potatoes would have pleased them better!
They didn't really like this kind of food at all.
Why did she do it? How would she feel about
it tonight, when she sank dead weary into bed,
after these stupid boys had said good-night, and
their yellow shoes had carried them down the
hill?

She was not eating anything, she was using up
all her vitality to electrify these heavy lads into
speech. Niel felt that he must help her, or at
least try to. He addressed them one after another with energy and determination; he tried
baseball, politics, scandal, the corn crop. They
answered him with monosyllables or exclama-
tions. He soon realized that they didn't want
his polite remarks; they wanted more duck, and
to be let alone with it.

Dinner was soon over, at any rate. The hostess' attempts to prolong it were unavailing.
The salad and frozen pudding were dispatched
as promptly as the roast had been. The guests
went into the parlour and lit cigars.

Mrs. Forrester had the old-fashioned notion
that men should be alone after dinner. She did
not join them for half an hour. Perhaps she
had lain down upstairs, for she looked a little

rested. The boys were talking now, discussing a camping trip Ed Elliot was going to take in the mountains. They were giving him advice about camp outfits, trout flies, mixtures to keep off mosquitoes.

"I'll tell you, boys," said Mrs. Forrester, when she had listened to them for a moment, "when I go back to California, I intend to have a summer cabin up in the Sierras, and I invite you, one and all, to visit me. You'll have to work for your keep, you understand; cut the firewood and bring the water and wash the pots and pans, and go out and catch fish for breakfast. Ivy can bring his gun and shoot game for us, and I'll bake bread in an iron pot, the old trappers' way, if I haven't forgotten how. Will you come?"

"You bet we will! You know those mountains by heart, I expect?" said Ed Elliot.

She smiled and shook her head. "It would take a life-time to do that, Ed, more than a life-time. The Sierras,—there's no end to them, and they're magnificent."

Niel turned to her. "Have you ever told the boys how it was you first met Captain Forrester in the mountains out there? If they haven't heard the story, I think they would like it."

"Really, would you? Well, once upon a time,

when I was a very young girl, I was spending the summer at a camp in the mountains, with friends of my father's."

She began there, but that was not the beginning of the story; long ago Niel had heard from his uncle that the beginning was a scandal and a murder. When Marian Ormsby was nineteen, she was engaged to Ned Montgomery, a gaudy young millionaire of the Gold Coast. A few weeks before the date set for their marriage, Montgomery was shot and killed in the lobby of a San Francisco hotel by the husband of another woman. The subsequent trial involved a great deal of publicity, and Marian was hurried away from curious eyes and sent up into the mountains until the affair should blow over.

Tonight Mrs. Forrester began with "Once upon a time." Sitting at one end of the big sofa, her slippers on a foot-stool and her head in shadow, she stirred the air before her face with the sandalwood fan as she talked, the rings glittering on her white fingers She told them how Captain Forrester, then a widower, had come up to the camp to visit her father's partner. She had noticed him very little,—she was off every day with the young men. One afternoon she had persuaded young Fred Harney, an intrepid mountain climber, to take her down the face of Eagle

Cliff. They were almost down, and were creep-
ing over a projecting ledge, when the rope broke,
and they dropped to the bottom. Harney fell on
the rocks and was killed instantly. The girl was
caught in a pine tree, which arrested her fall.
Both her legs were broken, and she lay in the
canyon all night in the bitter cold, swept by the
icy canyon draught. Nobody at the camp knew
where to look for the two missing members of
the party,—they had stolen off alone for their
foolhardy adventure. Nobody worried, because
Harney knew all the trails and could not get lost.
In the morning, however, when they were still
missing, search parties went out. It was Captain
Forrester's party that found Marian, and got her
out by the lower trail. The trail was so steep
and narrow, the turns round the jutting ledges
so sharp, that it was impossible to take her out
on a litter. The men took turns carrying her,
hugging the canyon walls with their shoulders as
they crept along. With her broken legs hang-
ing, she suffered terribly,—fainted again and
again. But she noticed that she suffered less
when Captain Forrester carried her, and that he
took all the most dangerous places on the trail
himself. "I could feel his heart pump and his
muscles strain," she said, "when he balanced himself and me on the rocks. I knew that if we fell,

we'd go together; he would never drop me."

They got back to camp, and everything possible was done for her, but by the time a surgeon could be got up from San Francisco, her fractures had begun to knit and had to be broken over again.

"It was Captain Forrester I wanted to hold my hand when the surgeon had to do things to me. You remember, Niel, he always boasted that I never screamed when they were carrying me up the trail. He stayed at the camp until I could begin to walk, holding to his arm. When he asked me to marry him, he didn't have to ask twice. Do you wonder?" She looked with a smile about the circle, and drew her finger-tips absently across her forehead as if to brush away something,—the past, or the present, who could tell?

The boys were genuinely moved. While she was answering their questions, Niel thought about the first time he ever heard her tell that story: Mr. Dalzell had stopped off with a party of friends from Chicago; Marshall Field and the president of the Union Pacific were among them, he remembered, and they were going through in Mr. Dalzell's private car to hunt in the Black Hills. She had, after all, not changed so much since then. Niel felt tonight that the right man could save her, even now. She was still her in-

domitable self, going through her old part,—
but only the stage-hands were left to listen to
her. All those who had shared in fine undertakings and bright occasions were gone.

IX

WITH the summer months Judge Pommeroy's health improved, and as soon
as he was able to be back in his office,
Niel began to plan to return to Boston. He
would get there the first of August and would go
to work with a tutor to make up for the months
he had lost. It was a melancholy time for him.
He was in a fever of impatience to be gone, and
yet he felt that he was going away forever, and
was making the final break with everything that
had been dear to him in his boyhood. The people, the very country itself, were changing so fast
that there would be nothing to come back to.

He had seen the end of an era, the sunset of
the pioneer. He had come upon it when already
its glory was nearly spent. So in the buffalo
times a traveller used to come upon the embers
of a hunter's fire on the prairie, after the hunter
was up and gone; the coals would be trampled
out, but the ground was warm, and the flattened
grass where he had slept and where his pony had
grazed, told the story.

This was the very end of the road-making

West; the men who had put plains and mountains under the iron harness were old; some were poor, and even the successful ones were hunting for rest and a brief reprieve from death. It was already gone, that age; nothing could ever bring it back. The taste and smell and song of it, the visions those men had seen in the air and followed,—these he had caught in a kind of afterglow in their own faces,—and this would always be his.

It was what he most held against Mrs. Forrester; that she was not willing to immolate herself, like the widow of all these great men, and die with the pioneer period to which she belonged; that she preferred life on any terms. In the end, Niel went away without bidding her good-bye. He went away with weary contempt for her in his heart.

It happened like this,—had scarcely the dignity of an episode. It was nothing, and yet it was everything. Going over to see her one summer evening, he stopped a moment by the dining-room window to look at the honeysuckle. The dining-room door was open into the kitchen, and there Mrs. Forrester stood at a table, making pastry. Ivy Peters came in at the kitchen door, walked up behind her, and unconcernedly put both arms around her, his hands meeting over her breast.

She did not move, did not look up, but went on rolling out pastry.

Niel went down the hill. "For the last time," he said, as he crossed the bridge in the evening light, "for the last time." And it was even so; he never went up the poplar-bordered road again. He had given her a year of his life, and she had thrown it away. He had helped the Captain to die peacefully, he believed; and now it was the Captain who seemed the reality. All those years he had thought it was Mrs. Forrester who made that house so different from any other. But ever since the Captain's death it was a house where old friends, like his uncle, were betrayed and cast off, where common fellows behaved after their kind and knew a common woman when they saw her.

If he had not had the nature of a spaniel, he told himself, he would never have gone back after the first time. It took two doses to cure him. Well, he had had them! Nothing she could ever do would in the least matter to him again.

He had news of her now and then, as long as his uncle lived. *"Mrs. Forrester's name is everywhere coupled with Ivy Peters',"* the Judge wrote. *"She does not look happy, and I fear her health is failing, but she has put herself in such a position that her husband's friends cannot help her."*

And again: *"Of Mrs. Forrester, no news is good news. She is sadly broken."*

After his uncle's death, Niel heard that Ivy Peters had at last bought the Forrester place, and had brought a wife from Wyoming to live there. Mrs. Forrester had gone West,—people supposed to California.

It was years before Niel could think of her without chagrin. But eventually, after she had drifted out of his ken, when he did not know if Daniel Forrester's widow were living or dead, Daniel Forrester's wife returned to him, a bright, impersonal memory.

He came to be very glad that he had known her, and that she had had a hand in breaking him in to life. He has known pretty women and clever ones since then,—but never one like her, as she was in her best days. Her eyes, when they laughed for a moment into one's own, seemed to promise a wild delight that he has not found in life. "I know where it is," they seemed to say, "I could show you!" He would like to call up the shade of the young Mrs. Forrester, as the witch of Endor called up Samuel's, and challenge it, demand the secret of that ardour; ask her whether she had really found some ever-bloom-ing, ever-burning, every-piercing joy, or whether it was all fine play-acting. Probably she had found no more than another; but she had always the power of suggesting things much lovelier than herself, as the perfume of a single flower may call up the whole sweetness of spring.

Niel was destined to hear once again of his long-lost lady. One evening as he was going into the dining-room of a Chicago hotel, a broad-shouldered man with an open, sunbrowned face, approached him and introduced himself as one of the boys who had grown up in Sweet Water.

"I'm Ed Elliott, and I thought it must be you. Could we take a table together? I promised an old friend of yours to give you a message, if I ever ran across you. You remember Mrs. Forrester? Well, I saw her again, twelve years after she left Sweet Water,—down in Buenos Ayres." They sat down and ordered dinner.

"Yes, I was in South America on business. I'm a mining engineer, I spent some time in Buenos Ayres. One evening there was a banquet of some sort at one of the big hotels, and I happened to step out of the bar, just as a car drove up to the entrance where the guests were going in. I paid no attention until one of the ladies laughed. I recognized her by her laugh,—that hadn't changed a particle. She was all done up in furs, with a scarf over her head, but I saw her eyes, and then I was sure. I stepped up and spoke to her. She seemed glad to see me, made me go into the hotel, and talked to me until her husband came to drag her away to the dinner. Oh, yes, she was married again,—to a rich, cranky old Englishman; Henry Collins was his name. He was born down there, she told me, but she met him in California. She told me they lived on a big stock ranch and had come down in their car for this banquet. I made inquiries afterward and found the old fellow was quite a character; had been married twice before, once to a Brazilian woman. People said he was rich, but quarrelsome and rather stingy. She seemed to have everything, though. They travelled in a fine French car, and she had brought her maid along, and he had his valet. No, she hadn't changed as much as you'd think. She was a good deal made up, of course, like most of the women down there; plenty of powder, and a little red, too, I guess. Her hair was black, blacker than I remembered it; looked as if she dyed it. She invited me to visit them on their estate, and so did the old man, when he came to get her. She asked about everybody, and said, 'If you ever meet Niel Herbert, give him my love, and tell him I often

—173—

think of him.' She said again, 'Tell him things have turned out well for me. Mr. Collins is the kindest of husbands.' I called at your office in New York on my way back from South America, but you were somewhere in Europe. It was remarkable, how she'd come up again. She seemed pretty well gone to pieces before she left Sweet Water."

"Do you suppose," said Niel, "that she could be living still? I'd almost make the trip to see her."

"No, she died about three years ago. I know that for certain. After she left Sweet Water, wherever she was, she always sent a cheque to the Grand Army Post every year to have flowers put on Captain Forrester's grave for Decoration Day. Three years ago the Post got a letter from the old Englishman, with a draft for the future care of Captain Forrester's grave, '*in memory of my late wife, Marian Forrester Collins.*'"

"So we may feel sure that she was well cared for, to the very end," said Niel. "Thank God for that!"

"I knew you'd feel that way," said Ed Elliot, as a warm wave of feeling passed over his face. "I did!"

WILLA CATHER (1873-1947) was born near Winchester, Virginia. When she was ten, her family moved from the peace of Virginia to the wild prairies of Nebraska. She was graduated from the University of Nebraska at twenty-one, and did newspaper work and teaching in Pittsburgh, Pennsylvania, for the next few years. She published a book of verse, April Twilights, in 1903, and a book of short stories, The Troll Garden, in 1905. They were followed, over the years, by twelve novels, including Death Comes for the Archbishop and Shadows on the Rock; four volumes of short stories, and two volumes of essays. Willa Cather was awarded the Pulitzer Prize for fiction in 1923.

VINTAGE BIOGRAPHY AND AUTOBIOGRAPHY

VINTAGE FICTION, POETRY, AND PLAYS

VINTAGE BELLES—LETTRES

VINTAGE CRITICISM: LITERATURE, MUSIC, AND ART

V-570   **ANDREWS, WAYNE** / American Gothic
V-418   **AUDEN, W. H.** / The Dyer's Hand
V-887   **AUDEN, W. H.** / Forewords and Afterwords
V-161   **BROWN, NORMAN O.** / Closing Time
V-75   **CAMUS, ALBERT** / The Myth of Sisyphus and Other Essays
V-626   **CAMUS, ALBERT** / Lyrical and Critical Essays
V-535   **EISEN, JONATHAN** / The Age of Rock: Sounds of the American Cultural Revolution
V-4   **EINSTEIN, ALFRED** / A Short History of Music
V-13   **GILBERT, STUART** / James Joyce's Ulysses
V-407   **HARDWICK, ELIZABETH** / Seduction and Betrayal: Women and Literature
V-114   **HAUSER, ARNOLD** / Social History of Art, Vol. I
V-115   **HAUSER, ARNOLD** / Social History of Art, Vol. II
V-116   **HAUSER, ARNOLD** / Social History of Art, Vol. III
V-117   **HAUSER, ARNOLD** / Social History of Art, Vol. IV
V-610   **HSU, KAI-YU** The Chinese Literary Scene
V-201   **HUGHES, H. STUART** / Consciousness and Society
V-88   **KERMAN, JOSEPH** / Opera as Drama
V-995   **KOTT, JAN** / The Eating of the Gods: An Interpretation of Greek Tragedy
V-685   **LESSING, DORIS** / A Small Personal Voice: Essays, Reviews, Interviews
V-677   **LESTER, JULIUS** / The Seventh Son, Vol. I
V-678   **LESTER, JULIUS** / The Seventh Son, Vol. II
V-720   **MIRSKY, D. S.** / A History of Russian Literature
V-118   **NEWMAN, ERNEST** / Great Operas, Vol. I
V-119   **NEWMAN, ERNEST** / Great Operas, Vol. II
V-976   **QUASHA, GEORGE AND JEROME ROTHENBERG (eds.)** America A Prophecy: A New Reading of American Poetry from Pre-Columbian Times to the Present
V-976   **ROTHENBERG, JEROME AND GEORGE QUASHA (eds.)** America A Prophecy: A New Reading of American Poetry from Pre-Columbian Times to the Present
V-415   **SHATTUCK, ROGER** / The Banquet Years, Revised
V-435   **SPENDER, STEPHEN** / Love-Hate Relations: English and American Sensibilities
V-278   **STEVENS, WALLACE** / The Necessary Angel
V-100   **SULLIVAN, J. W. N.** / Beethoven: His Spiritual Development
V-166   **SZE, MAI-MAI** / The Way of Chinese Painting
V-162   **TILLYARD, E. M. W.** / The Elizabethan World Picture